by the best selling author
Dennis WC Wong
Mansi
as Annalise
Neela
Dress Designer
Annalise's
Wish
Sequel of Arya
Published by
Sankalp Art

Copyright

Book Edited, Illustrated, Cover designed, Formatted, and Published by

SankalpArt

www.sankalpart.com

Author: Dennis W.C. Wong
Publisher: SankalpArt

Visit my website at https://www.denniswcwongauthor.com/
Printed in the United States of America

This book is dedicated to my wife, Jocelyn N. Wong

CONTENTS

INTRODUCTION

A time will come when we will want nothing but answers to questions that burden us, which we cannot decipher. At such times, we leave ourselves at the mercy of fate and providence, without even having the faintest idea of how things would eventually turn out.

Our total mortality, ingrained in our weakness, is exposed in such an instance. In the case of Lucinda's situation, many issues around her had been resolved, dousing her frayed nerves, but she still had unanswered questions yet to be addressed.

Annalise's Wish gives an in-depth explanation of Lucinda's and Annalise's birth circumstances. It tells the story of how women could go the extra mile to hold their bundle of joy and for someone to call them "mother". Children bring color to a dull family. They light up the whole room with joy and happiness with their arrival into this world. The plot takes a different twist, introducing Jake, who is the son of the sun and will be Lucinda's mate, hoping that their marriage will resolve the conflict between the two worlds.

"**Annalise's Wish**" is a sequel to " ***Anya*** " and it is part four of "***Over the Distant Mountain Ranges***", followed by "***Beyond the Ranges***."

I have provided some excerpts from the previous editions: She was named Lucinda, the daughter of a poor farmer. She was her parent's favorite and their only child. They didn't have all the good and pleasant things of life.

"Well, my parents lived on the mountain because of the calmness in that area, and nope, they don't have neighbors. I know the next question would be, how do they eat? They travel to the village close to them to get foodstuffs every Friday. That's all," Annalise replied.

There was an epidemic of flu spreading across the region, and so far, Lucinda was the only one out of the three members of this household that had not yet contracted it. Her parents were already down with the virus.

"Listen, Lucinda, this illness is spreading everywhere, and it' so contagious. I want you to go back to my parent's place," They were sick, and they didn't let anyone know. Now her parents are gone.

"Lucinda, it's me. My soul lives in this horse, "The white horse said.

"She isn't just the only one. Your father is here too" The brown horse said.

"Since your soul lives in this white horse, I will call you Annalise, and since Dad lives in this brown horse, I will call him Phil," Lucinda said.

One won't even guess there was something under the bed or hidden in that old box. Maya unlocked it and opened it up as she brought out the seashell.

Lucinda felt something substantial as soon as she touched the seashell.

"Our grandchild is special. She is a young child filled with wisdom who doesn't act her age. Yes, she understands the language of the horses. Lucinda, your grandchild, spends quality time with the horses because her parents' spirit lives in the horses, and she is the only one who can hear them. Just let her be as she is bonding with

her parents, and she barely has enough time because eventually, they will be gone forever," The old woman said.

"Lucinda, we were only given five years grace to stay with you here on earth, and the timelapses on your 15th birthday," Phil explained.

"I understand how you feel, Lucinda. We were given the privilege to communicate with you. But unfortunately, you can never see us again. So, let's be content with our voices. I have been here a couple of times. After your fifteenth birthday, I had no choice but to decide to relocate to the city with you so you could forget what happened. I was able to buy this with the little savings we have, and here we are now." Greg replied.

"You are the queen. You invited your subject over here. You asked me to come. Your presence in this city woke me up, yet you can't summon the courage to talk to your subject." The voice persisted.

"Anya is three in one, an amalgam of the sort, both a deadly beast and a wonderful soul. So, you choose which side of her you want." Mia replied.

"I am the goddess of this river, and I know more because I have existed for ages and ages. When you were drowning in this place years ago, I didn't want to kill you; I only wanted to show you a little about your life, but Phil came in time to save you. The moon and stars have waited for a long time, and they want their daughter to fix this as ordained."; Mia replied as she walked into the river, and before Lucinda could say anything, she vanished before her sight.

"But you are not like them; you're different. You're a queen crowned even before your birth. Your life was meant to be different, and no matter how you wish for it, your life is perfect." Anya replied.

"My name is Lucia, daughter of the moon and the stars. You're my incarnation. The people are torturing the people I would do anything for at any cost to protect and me." Lucia replied.

Anya couldn't believe that Lucinda was ever going to kneel and bow before her. Now there was no way she was going to hurt anyone again. Anya knew that whatever she needed must be granted once the queen bowed to her. That act of Lucinda's humility has hindered her.

"*All the answers you seek are in the Book of Prophecy; it holds every story you need to know; prophecies that were given before your birth*," Amber replied.

"*I'm the seer who has reincarnated four times now. I was here when you were as the other queen and was killed, but I never got to see her face. The same queen is you. You're back again; just that it took you long to come back to earth. So, I kept reincarnating, hoping that I would someday be opportune to see the queen, and here I am today, standing right next to her.*" Amber said, smiling.

"*The bracelet is from my grandmother; I can't remove it. She is just like my mother, and as for the necklace, it's a gift from Anya. It was the necklace that unlocked the book.*" Lucinda replied, sighing.

◆ ◆ ◆

CHAPTER ONE

She knew her mom made a wish, but what prompted her to make the wish remained a mystery to her. Indeed, something must have happened, and she needed to know. Indeed, these questions could only be answered by her mom, Annalise.

As Lucinda lay on her bed, different shades of thoughts were racing through her mind. She was restless, tossing and turning on her bed.

Looking through the window, she saw the stars in the sky shining so bright. In the darkness are the chirping of the crickets, the hooting of the owls, and the neighing of the horses in the stable.

She waited and remained awake into the deep hours of the night, and when she was sure that her grandparents were asleep, she disappeared from the house, reappearing at their meeting place, but they weren't there yet, so she just sat down and waited for them. She waited for midnight, the very time of their meeting.

It didn't take long before it was midnight, and just like always, Annalise and Phil came out together from the nearby bush, having Amber and Anya in their tow.

After exchanges of greetings and fraternal hugging, they started playing a game of Jumanji. Still, throughout it, everyone noticed Lucinda was absent-minded, and that something was bothering her.

"You seem off. What could be the problem?" Amber asked.

"You know the least you can do is only to ask whenever you think you need answers to anything," Anya added.

"Lucinda, what's the problem? You know you can always talk to us. Something is bothering you, and it is even written all over your face. We need you to be happy so we can be happy too. Please talk to us. You need to." Phil pleaded.

"Something has been bothering me. You are right. I need to get answers based on what Grandpa told me about Mom's wish before birth. But I think there is more to it." Lucinda said.

"What do you mean, my child?" Annalise asked.

"It's all about the circumstances surrounding my birth. I need to know more about my birth. I need to know how I came back as the daughter of the moon and the stars and what prompted you to make the wish you made in promising to dedicate me to the moon and the stars.

I know I might be asking for too much, but you will lift the burden off my shoulders if you tell me everything I need to know." Lucinda said, clearly worried.

"Alright, I will tell you, but that shouldn't get you so worried. You only needed to ask." Annalise said.

"Alright, I'm all ears," Lucinda said, shifting slightly on the ground.

FLASHBACK

Annalise could be seen throwing pebbles into the river as tears dripped down her cheeks. Something was wrong somewhere. She couldn't even express herself. She was short of words about what to say. The only thing left in her were her tears, which she freely allowed to do the talking.

"Why has the world decided to be unfair to me? What offense have I committed against the universe that she feels is the right way to punish me? Am I not fit to be called a mother? Why can't I birth a child? The most annoying part is not that the pregnancies aren't coming. They are, but it will be gone once I take in less than three months." Annalise whined within herself, sobbing gently.

Phil, who had been looking for Annalise, had to check at the riverside to see if she would be there, and luckily, he found her there.

On seeing Annalise, Phil was sad, noting the dire state, but she couldn't do anything.

He had tried talking to her several times, reminding her he would love her wholeheartedly with or without a child, but Annalise wouldn't hear of that.

They had been married for two years now, and none of the pregnancies had lasted for over three months. Annalise wanted to carry her child. She wanted to be called a mother.

"Annalise, please let's go home." Phil pleaded.

"Home? That place isn't home. There is nothing special about there to be called my home. How can that place be called home when there is no child to cuddle or call me mom?

Maybe it's time for the universe to explain why they are unfair to me. She has to tell me what's wrong with me. She should tell me so I can apologize and be given a chance to be a mother. I'm tired of this pain and humiliation. I want to be a mother, even if it is just one child. Phil, we have been married for two years and six months, and until today, the cry of a baby hasn't been heard in this family. I feel so empty. The universe has a lot of answers for me, I think. I need to know my offense today." Annalise said with a teary voice.

"My dear, it's okay. I understand your condition. I fully understand the situation. A child will come when the time is right. Perhaps not now, but later in the future." Phil said.

"Future? The future is now. I want that child now, or better still, they should open up to me and tell me what I did wrong; so I can have a baby, my baby." Annalise shrieked.

"Things don't work like that, Annalise. Listen. I will love you with or without a child until the end of time. It would be best if you stopped killing yourself over this issue. I have seen couples who had children after a decade of marriage.

You just need to exercise more patience. A child will come when the time is right, and even if a child doesn't come, I will still love you, and I won't marry anyone else. I swear on my life, Annalise. This isn't the Annalise I married." Phil said bitterly.

"You're right. This Annalise you married has changed so much. Deprivation of life, pain, and anger have changed me so much, yet I disagree that it's my fault. All I ever wanted was just a child, not even riches or material things. I just want to experience the joy of motherhood. I'm not selfish to ask of that, but I don't understand why the universe has refused to give me a child despite my countless pleas. I know the universe can hear me, but I don't know why they are silent. For how long will I keep languishing in this pain and misery? For how long, Phil? Haven't I waited long enough? I'm not others. I don't have to wait for a decade before I can be blessed with a child," Annalise said with a teary voice.

Phil sat beside her, stroked her hair a bit, and rested her head on his shoulders. They were like that for a long time, and when Phil made sure Annalise had calmed down, he drew her up while standing up before they strolled down to the house. Phil helped to prepare something to eat as Annalise took her bath. Before Phil could finish up and walk into the room with the food, Annalise was already fast asleep.

Phil wouldn't wake her up. He just had to cover her up adequately because of the cold weather as he sat staring at his wife. The quest for a child was driving Annalise insane. She was now completely different, and she didn't even care about herself anymore. Annalise kept screaming out that she wanted a child. Despite Phil's love and reassuring words, Annalise still won't give up as the only thing that could ever restore her joy would be when she gives birth to her child. Yet, Phil loved Annalise so much more than anything else in this world, with or without the child.

It was already 5 pm when Annalise woke up from sleep. Phil had to warm the food up and serve Annalise. She ate half portion and told Phil she was full. There was simply no appetite for her.

"But you haven't eaten anything since morning," Phil said.

"Don't worry; I'm fine," Annalise said.

Phil stood up as he took the plates and dropped them in the sink, after which he came back later and sat close to Annalise.

"Phil, can I talk to you about something?" Annalise asked.

"Sure, what's that?" Phil asked.

"Do you see me as someone who has lost her sanity?" Annalise asked.

"No, but why will you even say that?" Phil asked.

"It's because of my daily rants of not having a baby of mine," Annalise replied.

"It's normal; any woman in your shoes will act the same way, and I won't blame you for anything. I just want you to know that despite everything that is happening, I still love you, and I will love you till the end of time, but I just want you to promise me one thing." Phil said.

"What's that?" Annalise asked.

"I just want my old Annalise back. I would do anything to see that smile again. I don't like this new Annalise, the new Annalise that has tied her happiness to childbirth. I can't even remember the last time I saw you smile. But, please, I want you to smile and be happy always.

I know things will change soon. I just want you to be patient. Things will work out soon, okay?" Phil pleaded.

"Even though it's tough, I will try to smile even amidst these tribulations.

I wish things could change, and I would be blessed with a child. I promise to love and protect this child until the day my eyelids close in death. Even in death, I will watch over her and be with her always." Annalise said.

"Her! Do you also want a girl child?" Phil asked.

"Amazing! You also wish to have a girl child!" Annalise said as Phil smiled. Phil wanted his wife to be happy and to experience motherhood.

"Don't worry. Your wish will be granted to you soon enough. Just have faith." Phil said.

They both discussed it at length that evening. Annalise was the first to show that she was feeling sleepy. Phil covered her up as he watched her doze off. It didn't take time before Phil dozed off as well.

It was five years now as the couple kept hoping for a child, though Annalise tried to act strong. Phil knew his wife was upset.

Phil had gone to the town to sell off some items they weren't using at home. It was already 6 pm, and Phil wasn't back yet.

So, Annalise sat on the balcony as she patiently waited for her husband. As she looked up to the sky, she saw the incandescence of the moon, and the sky was filled with stars.

"They look so beautiful," Annalise said, smiling as her eyes were fixated on the starry sky.

"I wish I had a child who will sit with me and admire the beautiful scenery of the sky, a child who shines brighter than the stars in the sky, a child that even the moon would obey. I wish the moon and the stars will hear this woman's voice who wants nothing but a child. I wish my heart's desires will be granted to me." Annalise said as she smiled.

Annalise's eyes were still fixed on the sky when someone tapped her, and that was when she noticed Phil was back.

"I can see that you are admiring nature. The sky looks breathtaking today," Phil said.

"Yeah, it looks wonderful. I feel these stars came out today just because of me. I think they heard my voice, my cry, and my pain, and they are here to fix everything." Annalise said with a smile on her face.

"I hope so. Let's go inside." Phil said as he led his wife inside the house. They ate dinner, after which Phil took his bath before he retired to the bedroom.

After the incident of her last wish, it became apparent to Annalise that she was pregnant, four months counting, but she didn't want to tell her husband. She felt this wasn't going to last. She thought it was going to leave the same way others left.

Annalise was sleeping on the bed that afternoon when Phil tapped her, and she slowly opened her eyes.

"Annalise, can you sit up? I want to ask you a question." Phil said as Annalise sat up slowly.

"When do you plan on telling me, or do you think you will keep it hidden forever? I don't understand." Phil said.

"What do you mean?" Annalise said, feigning ignorance.

"The pregnancy. It's four months, Annalise," Phil said.

"Well, you already know the answer. This will still go the same way others went. I will have a miscarriage soon. I'm already used to it. No pregnancy of mine, stay. So, what makes you think that this will be different?" Annalise said with a teary voice.

"Remember the wish you made," Phil said.

"What wish? I have made countless wishes, so what has it to do with this?" Annalise asked.

"The wish you made to the moon and the stars. Who knows if the universe heard you that day, and they have granted your wish." Phil said.

"But this; I'm not too sure," Annalise said.

"Wait and see, and please be positive. " Phil said.

"Thank you for never giving up on me and always standing by me. It's been five years now, but you are still with me here. So many men out there would have left, but you didn't. Instead, you stood by with me. I hope I will get to pay you back someday." Annalise said.

"You're my wife; that's enough of a price already," Phil said, smiling.

Despite Phil's assuring words, Annalise had her doubts that the pregnancy would not stay for long, but she was surprised when she got to her last trimester.

She sent words to her parents, which prompted their instant visit to see her for themselves. For five years, they had waited.

When they saw Annalise and Phil brimming with joy and happiness, they joined in their joyous mood. But they didn't stay long as they couldn't exchange any home for their home beyond the mountain ranges. They came in the morning, and they were already on their way home by evening.

When they left, Annalise went to the balcony to sit down and savor the glittering sky filled with twinkling stars.

"I made a mere wish because of the agony in my heart, and somehow you heard it, and you granted that wish to me. I don't know what else to say but thank you. I'm grateful. Today for the first time in five years, I have been able to carry pregnancy till the seventh month, showing that this baby has come to stay.

I will name her Lucinda.

That's the only name I can think of, and I think that's the proper name that suits the daughter of the moon and the stars.

Nations will bow under her. She will rule nations of men and women with the special gifts.

I never got to enjoy all the things as a child, and even now, she will have them in ten folds as an adult.

I'm not making a wish this time. I'm only stating how my daughter's life will be because she has wiped my tears away and proven to all that I'm a woman." Annalise said as she kept caressing her stomach while smiling.

"***Lucinda***, *that's the name I have given to you today. You will be born to us, poor fellows, but trust me, nations will bow down before your feet. I don't know how that will happen, but I can feel it will happen.*" Annalise said, smiling as she stood up and went inside.

On the day that Annalise gave birth, they heard the howling of the wolves, but instead of being worried about that, Phil and Annalise joked about it.

"Their queen is here, so they need to pay some respect," Phil said, laughing.

"***Even though we haven't heard the howls of the wolves before, today we heard it loud and clear, which shows that the universe has acknowledged the birth of my child***," Annalise said, smiling.

"Can you see how beautiful the sky is? The stars are even shining brighter. So indeed, their daughter is home." Phil said as they both looked at their tiny baby and smiled.

****

"So, you see, this is the story of your conception, and that was why I was very overprotective, and I wouldn't want you to get close to the river because I waited for five years before I could have you. I wouldn't want any harm to befall you." Annalise said.

"It was a tough time for us, but I'm glad somehow the wish your mom made was granted unto her. Somehow, I felt like the universe was waiting for her to make that wish. It sounds weird, but it's like that was what happened." Phil said.

"Are Grandma and Grandpa aware of this?" Lucinda asked, keeping quiet for some time.

"They were not aware of everything I went through because I tried to keep a happy face each time they visited, and they didn't suspect that anything was wrong. But my dad was around the day I made the wish to the moon and the stars, though he didn't understand the main reason why I did that." Annalise said.

"That explains why Grandpa knows little about my birth. I

wanted a full story. That's why I had to ask you. I already knew about the wish, but I didn't know why you made that wish. I'm okay with the answers now." Lucinda said.

"Deep down, you still have more questions though you're yet to put the questions together. I hope you find all the answers that you seek." Amber said as Lucinda looked at her and smiled, slightly nodding her head in acknowledgment.

Amber was right. Lucinda still had so many questions, but she didn't know how to put them all together. One thing was sure, her parents did not have answers to the remaining questions.

"It's time," Phil said as Lucinda watched her parents slowly fade away with Amber.

"I wish they could stay longer. I wish they don't have to go every 3 am. But why can't they stay without leaving? Why is it not possible?" Lucinda said.

"I don't know, Lucinda. I don't have the answer to that question, but trust me, it will come to you when you need the answers." Anya said, then, looking at Lucinda straight in the eyes added: "You have changed so much. You're growing older and wiser. I'm happy for you."

"Thank you so much. I hope someday I'll see what the other world looks like." Lucinda said.

"Soon," Anya said as she slowly turned into a wolf, and before Lucinda could say anything, she was already inside the woods.

"Too many mysteries to be unveiled and too many questions to be answered. I hope I find all the answers to these riddles that needed to be solved. I'm going to find out everything, and I will fix everything that needs to be fixed. I hope I get enough time to do all that." Lucinda said within herself.

◆ ◆ ◆

CHAPTER TWO

As Lucinda laid in her bed, she started recalling and trying to rationalize the circumstances surrounding her birth as was told to her by her mom. She recalled that her mom said she was tired of losing her pregnancies through miscarriages and that after five years, when all hope was lost, she made a wish to the moon and the stars, which was granted.

The moon and the stars chose to send her back to earth through Annalise. But then, what could have happened if Annalise hadn't made any wish? If not for her, wouldn't her mom have given birth to anyone? Were the moon and the stars responsible for her mom's repeated miscarriages?

Lucinda concluded there was more to the story than her mom told her. And clearly, Annalise didn't know more than she narrated. She was a simple rural woman whose only wish was to have a baby girl.

Looking out into the night through her windows, Lucinda was determined to find answers to these. Soon after chewing these thoughts in her mind, she drifted off to sleep after covering herself with thick clothes.

Hardly had Lucinda woken up the following day when she heard a faint knock on her door, and on getting up, she gently opened the door to see her grandmother standing at the door with hands akimbo. Not that she was angry with Lucinda, but that was her manner of standing most of the time.

"Lucinda, it's already 10 am, and you're still asleep. Is everything okay because I know you went to bed early?" Maya asked.

"Yeah, Grandma, I'm okay. I will be out in a few minutes; just let me take my bath." Lucinda said.

"Alright, we will be waiting for you," Maya said as she walked out.

Lucinda closed her door quietly and sat back on the bed. She started thinking about her life. Rummaging through her entire life, especially her communication with her dead parents, she became tired of hiding things from her grandparents.

Lucinda tried to find out the whole truth about herself. She wanted to know everything her birth and her motive to be in this life. Lucinda knew that she had to act if she would ever get to the bottom of the riddle. Next, she stood up, walked into her bathroom, and quickly showered before wearing her clothes.

"Where is Grandpa?" Lucinda asked.

"Oh, he went out, but he will soon be back. He went to the next town to see a friend." Maya replied.

"A friend? I've never heard Grandpa mention anything about having a friend, so how come this sudden he was going to see a friend today?" Lucinda asked, eyeing Maya.

"Lucinda, you must not know everything. Your food is in the kitchen, go and eat." Maya said as Lucinda glanced at her for a split second before going to the kitchen to eat her food.

She carried the food back to the sitting room and sat on the chair close to her grandma.

Maya noticed how Lucinda was picking at her food, and it was apparent that something was wrong with her. She knew how Lucinda preferred keeping things to herself. No matter how hard one tried, she would never talk to anyone concerning her problems, but she decided just to ask, as she couldn't go on pretending that all was well with her granddaughter sitting next to her.

"Lucinda," Maya called.

"Yes, Grandma," Lucinda replied.

"Is everything okay? Don't tell me yes; because you have been picking your food, and I'm certain something is wrong somewhere. Listen, you know that Greg and I love you so much, and in as much as we want to be part of your happiness, we also want to be part of your sadness. Whatever troubles you also trouble us.

So, please tell me, what's bothering you? You have been moody even when I walked into your room. Something is eating you up. What is it?" Maya asked in a most solemn voice.

"Well, Grandma, I feel there are questions I deserve to know the answers to and I don't know if I will ever get the answers," Lucinda replied.

"And what could those questions be? If I had answers to your questions, I know I would answer you. I want you to be happy because you are all we have here." Maya said.

"My mom. I mean your daughter, Annalise," Lucinda said.

"What happened to her?" Maya asked.

"I know she is your daughter, and I know she is dead, but I don't want to bring up bad memories. I'm just seeking answers. That's all." Lucinda said.

"Okay, tell me, what is the problem?" Maya asked.

"Did you have any challenges before you gave birth to my mom? Were there any unusual or unnatural circumstances surrounding her birth and even conception? I just need to know what happened before and after she was conceived and given birth." Lucinda asked.

"Why do you need to know?" Maya asked after some momentary silence from her.

"I know it will be hard on you to tell me everything, but I need to know. It will help me solve certain riddles, but don't bother asking what they are because I won't tell you. It is when I must have fixed everything I can. I will explain but for now, tell me everything I need to know." Lucinda pleaded.

"Annalise is my only child. She was my first fruit that lived, but she wasn't the first seed that opened my womb. Others came before her, but just that they didn't stay up to three months.

They died during the second month of all the pregnancies. I

became tired. I was even afraid of getting pregnant since I knew they wouldn't come to fruition. What was the need to get pregnant in the first place? It was like hell to me. Depression set in.

I became melancholic. I became desperate, so desperate that I made a wish on a certain night, a wish I believe solved whatever problem it was that was stopping me from getting pregnant because after that, I became pregnant, and it stayed. When I was delivered of a baby girl, I named her Annalise." Maya said.

"Wait, wait. You too made a wish, and why, please?" Lucinda asked, shifting a bit on her seat.

"Yes, I made a wish. I pleaded with the universe, the stars, the moon to give me even if it's just one child, and my wish was granted. I was delighted, but unfortunately, my happiness didn't last for long. It was ruined the day you ran to the mountain top to tell us they were no more. I had begged for that child, Annalise.

I had waited for years to conceive her. She was the only fruit I had here on earth, the only one who made me experience the joy of motherhood. She was the only child who made me a full woman.

I was angry with the universe that she took just one child she blessed me with, knowing full well the circumstances surrounding her birth, knowing the pain and hurdles I went through before I gave birth to her. But then, I had to console myself that I had you, and I swore to be there for you always.

Anytime I look at you, I see Annalise. I know I might never fill that vacuum created in your heart by her demise, but I promise to make you happy in any way I can. That was the same promise

I made to Annalise even before I gave birth to her, that I would love and care for all her children. Sadly, she isn't here today, but I'm happy that I'm trying in my little way to make you happy, Lucinda." Maya said, casting her head down in gloom.

"Well, you're right about not being able to fill the vacuum that has been created in my heart, but the truth remains that you and Grandpa are the second-best things that have happened to me here on earth and I'm happy that despite all the weird attitudes I have shown in the past, you both are still standing strong with me," Lucinda said.

"Anything for you, Lucinda, anything," Maya said.

"Now, Grandma, can you tell me everything I need to know about my mom's birth? Why did nature make you wait that long because, I mean, people are easily getting pregnant and being delivered babies daily? So, why would your own be different?" Lucinda said, dropping her food.

FLASHBACK

Maya was sitting down on the balcony discussing with her friend Martha who was breastfeeding her child.

"Your baby looks beautiful," Maya observed, smiling.

"You're a beautiful woman. I know your children will be beautiful as well." Martha replied.

"Maybe, but I don't know why life has decided to be unfair to me. I have been trying to give birth to my babies for the past five years, but it all ended in stillbirths. It's been five years of a childless marriage with Greg, my husband. It hurts.

I wish I could get to carry my children and breastfeed them. But even if it is just one seed, I will be grateful. I want to experience the joy of motherhood." Maya said with a teary voice.

"I already told you, don't worry. Children will come at the right time. You don't have to kill yourself for anything. My baby girl here, Lynn, is also your child. Please don't worry so much. Things will work out soon. I'm certain that you will carry your child someday. I'm not telling you this to comfort you, but I'm telling you this because it will happen soon." Martha said.

"How soon, Martha? Just how soon? It's been five years now!" Maya almost exclaimed.

"Don't worry, soon. You will be surprised when it happens. Trust me." Martha said.

"I hope so. I hope the child comes sooner," Maya said, revealing a wry smile, though laden with sadness.

It was already evening when Martha signified that she was ready to leave. Maya saw her off and returned home. Her husband Greg wasn't back yet, so she went into the garden to pluck some vegetables.

"Hey Maya! the way you to tend to this garden and eat the fruit it brings forth. Why don't you tend to yourself that way and bring forth fruit? Oh, now I remember, you can't. You are just a barren old hag who will never bear any fruit into this life." It was the voice of Cecilia, her neighbor shouting from her window nearby. Maya has been going through this for the past three years since she fell out with her neighbor. Since then, she had seized every opportunity to taunt her and remind her of her childlessness.

"Why are you mute? You can't say anything because that's the truth. You're a witch. Only witches don't give birth and eat their children while still in the womb, just like you. I wish Martha would stop visiting you before you kill her child." Her neighbor shouted again while laughing hysterically.

Maya picked up the vegetables as she silently walked out of the garden, but on second thought, she turned back and said, "You have made a mockery of me because of my condition. You have taunted me a whole lot and have called me barren and a witch. I hope nature steals that smile from your face someday. I hope nature places you in the same condition that I am in now. Only then can you realize the pain and agony of a childless woman."

In ennui did Maya make those proclamations, after which she went inside and straight to the kitchen to prepare dinner. She wasn't going to let what Cecilia said to get to her. One thing was sure to her that she would reap all that she had ever uttered to her in mockery someday.

When Greg got home, he noticed that Maya seemed a little off, and after eating and having her night bath, he called her and asked her why she was looking gloomy.

"What else could it be? Cecilia wouldn't have the guts to mock me if I had a child. She just mocked me again today, asking me to bear fruits, not eat the fruits from my garden. I was just on my own, and when she saw me from her window, she started talking rubbish to me. I'm not even asking for children.

Just one is enough to prove to everyone that I'm a woman, just one child so I can experience the joy of motherhood. Is that asking for too much? I need to know. I'm tired. I'm tired of waiting. I have waited for five years and nothing to show for it. Not only that the pregnancy isn't coming, it only comes to mock me. Haven't I suffered enough? Haven't I gotten enough punishment from the universe?

When will she hear my cries and give me a child? When will she shut the mouth of those who have mocked me and called me barren? Greg, tells me what I am living for because this life isn't making sense. Nothing matters anymore. If I can't have a child to call my own. I don't think I am meant to stay in the world. Maybe I need to go on a long sleep, end the pain, and be free from this endless pain, and mockery." Maya said, tearing up as she stood up to leave, but Greg held her hands as she sat back down.

"Are you giving up on everything? Are you giving up on me? For the first time since the challenge of giving birth to a child, you have talked and thought about death. That's suicidal. Do you want to go and leave everything that we both shared here on earth?

Do you want to leave without fulfilling those promises you made to me? Remember that you said you would be with me till the end of time? Why then do you want to leave? Why do you let people's talk get to you, even influence you into making a rash decision?

Doing so will only allow them to see you as a weakling, yet I know you're not weak, but a strong woman. Maya, I need to remind you of this. Perhaps you have forgotten. You will have a child. It's certain, maybe not now but very soon. So, you don't need to keep worrying yourself over what people say.

The miracle that will shut their mouth is going to happen very soon.

Just have faith, and don't lose hope. Don't let them see this weak side of you. Remain the strong woman you are, Maya," Greg said as he hugged her tightly.

They both retired to bed that night, but immediately it struck midnight. Maya woke up and went straight to the window. She stayed silent for a long time before she started declaring some words at the height of her bitterness, desperation, and pent-up emotions.

"I'm not barren, neither am I a witch. My day will come, and I know it. I don't know long I have to wait for this special gift.

The universe, I hope you can hear me. The stars and the moon in the sky, I hope you can hear me. I just wish to have my child, even if it is just one child. I want a child who will call me mother and call my husband father. I'm not asking for too much. I do not wish for something impossible.

I wish for things that happen every day in the lives of other women. I can't sleep. My heart is heavy. My soul is bitter and my heart is aching. I have realized that the only thing that can stop all of these is only when I hear the cry of my child. I hope the universe, the moon, the stars, and all the elements of this earth tend to this heart before it loses its thirst for life." Maya said as she sighed and went back to bed.

Days turned into weeks, weeks into months, months into years, and it was already ten years now, but Maya didn't stop. Every night she would make a wish to the universe and to the moon and the stars to give her a child.

And in a month, Maya suspected that she was pregnant again. When she knew she was pregnant, she made it a point of duty every night to wish for the child's safety. She kept making wishes every night till the day she gave birth to a baby girl. Greg and Maya were the happiest humans on earth that night because their bundle of joy arrived safely.

Martha was happy for her friend Maya. She helped the new parents out in the little way she could because she knew this was Maya's first baby, and she would need all the help she could get.

At last, Maya no longer cried every night. She was happy that at least her wish was granted. Finally, she had her child, someone who could call her mother.

Maya loved Annalise so much as she was the answer to the prayers that she had made for the past ten years. She was so happy that the universe had finally remembered her. And yes, she was the most beautiful baby. People would come to see her, then tell others of the baby's beauty. Her eyes twinkled like stars.

Maya and Greg made sure that Annalise always had a smile on her face as they wouldn't want to see her cry or sad. This was the child they waited ten years for, and now that she was here, they would treasure her for the rest of their lives.

****

"On the night that Annalise was born, something tragic happened. Cecilia lost her three children that same day. They all slept and never woke up. She lost her home and her husband. She lost everything."

How? Lucinda asked.

I don't know what happened, but I knew nature has a way of punishing wicked people. The truth is that I was not the only one she mocked. She mocked many people, and in return, all she got were curses from them. Cecilia left, and no one ever saw her again.

She didn't die or commit suicide, though; she still lived close to the mountains. No one sympathized with her because she had done nothing but cause pain to different people. I feel karma paid her back by taking all her children. Now she has no home, no husband, or even someone to call a child. She ruined herself." Maya said, looking calm and at peace with herself.

"So that's it. Even Annalise waited for so long. I thought she had the same issue with me, but she would always assure me that she and Phil would give birth when they were ready.

After I gave birth to Annalise, it felt like my womb was closed again, but I was so grateful that I already had her. She proved to be more than just a girl child. She did work meant for boys and she would do everything to make us happy.

We would do anything to make her happy. I was so attached to her that I didn't let her out of my sight for a second. I took her to visit her grandparents, ensuring we returned the same day.

That is the same way she always wanted you close to her. The bond was beyond the natural, perhaps, all thanks to your grandfather, who made me realize that Annalise wasn't truly gone, and you're the reflection of Annalise. Anything I do for you today would have done the same to Annalise if she was still here. I would kill myself if anything happens to you, Lucinda," Maya said, almost on the verge of tears.

Lucinda stood up as she walked closer to where Maya was sitting and hugged her tightly as she whispered comforting words to her, "Nothing will happen to me. I have come to stay, and I hope someday I will reunite you with your daughter, Annalise."

"What did you just say?" Maya said, looking at Lucinda bewildered.

"You heard me, Grandma, and don't think it is impossible. She is my mother too. Nothing is impossible in my world where I rule." Lucinda said, smiling as she picked up her plate of food and walked into her room. She wanted to eat alone.

Lucinda walked into her room, sat down, and ate her food slowly. She kept the remaining food by her bedside as she recollected everything her grandmother told her, every bit of it.

"This is interesting. My grandmother had my mother through a wish, the same way my mother had. Then why did my mother die? Why wasn't she the daughter of the moon and the stars like me? Why did the mantle rest on me?" Lucinda wondered as she tried to figure out what might have gone wrong.

"Only one person has an answer to this question, and I need to know why she wasn't the one to be made queen," Lucinda said as she stood up to lock her door, after which she closed her eyes to summon Amber.

"You called." As Lucinda opened her eyes to see Amber sitting on her bed, the voice said.

"I have some questions to ask and you should have the answers," Lucinda said.

"I agree that I'm a deer who has lived for thousands of years but be assured that I do not have all the answers to things that concern the other world," Amber replied.

"You should have an answer to this. This is about my mom," Lucinda said.

"And what about your mom?" Amber asked.

"My grandmother had my mom through a wish, experiencing the same thing that my mom experienced. Though mom didn't mention that she also went through the same thing. Grandma

pleaded to the moon and stars for a child, and her wish was granted, but something was off. ***Why wasn't my mom fit to hold the crown?*** She is also the daughter of the moon and the stars.
Why did they let her die?" Lucinda asked.

"Our destinies are tied to different things. You didn't know who you were until you came into the city." Amber said.

"That's true; it all started from Anya, and now I have realized my true being," Lucinda said.

"Let me make you understand something. It was in this very town that your grandma made that wish. I guess she didn't tell you that. Your mom Annalise was given birth to here, and after a few months, your grandparents moved out, and they went to the village mountain top to live. Maybe if they had stayed and waited for the full blood moon, the initiation would have been completed, the crown would have rested on your mom's head, and somehow her death would have been averted." Amber replied.

"This is confusing. But my mom made a wish while she was still in the village, and that's where she gave birth to me. So how come I didn't realize who I am until I got here?" Lucinda asked.

"The wish that brought your mom to earth was made right here in this city, and somehow fate drew you back here for you to complete the initiation. Your mom is also the daughter of the moon and the stars.

Even though she made her wish right there in the village, fate brought you back to your mother's roots.

Your grandma made the wish, but the initiation wasn't complete. Everything was fixed. Aside from the fact that you're a daughter of the moon and stars, the main reason why your mom and dad can still talk to you is that they are not full mortals and before you ask about your dad, the day he got married to your mom was the day he officially became the son of the moon and the stars." Amber said as she looked around.

"What's the problem?" Lucinda asked.

"I think it's time to go. The water is drying up. I have answered the questions which you want. I need to return home." Amber said.

"You can't go now. I need to know why my parents had to die if both of them were tied to the moon and stars. Why weren't they protected? Why did they let them die?" Lucinda asked, almost on the verge of tears.

"You can't blame anyone. Just like I said, the initiation wasn't complete before she was taken out of the city, which means she was vulnerable to attacks. Your grandma isn't to be blamed because she wasn't aware of the gravity of the wish she made. She knew that nature was kind enough to hear her pleas and helped her with one child.

And since your mom was tied to the village, her wombs were closed. That's why she experienced several miscarriages.

Since she wasn't in the town to complete her initiation, someone from her loins had to take over the crown that was left hanging there. They wanted her to call on the moon and the stars like her mother did.

If she had given birth freely, the moon and the stars wouldn't acknowledge the baby as theirs because it's not from them. That's why their wish had to be made, and somehow, she made that wish.

That's why you have the birthmarks of the shapes of moon and stars on your body, showing where you came from. They didn't lock her womb because of the mistake your grandmother made; rather, they did that because her lineage was found worthy and pure to bear the queen that rules the other word, and that's you, Lucinda," Amber said.

"It all makes sense now. The wish. It's all about the wish. So that's why everything started happening after I came to this town. They did not know the significance of the wish they both made." Lucinda said, nodding in understanding.

"My time is up. I need to go home now." Amber said as she slowly faded into thin air, leaving some golden dust on the bed and floor.

Lucinda took her plate with the unfinished food and unlocked her door. She went to the kitchen to wash the plate, after which she kept it in the dish rack with the other dishes. She then came out to see her grandpa conversing with her grandmother.

"You're back," Lucinda remarked.

"Yes, I am," Greg replied.

"You don't look happy. What's the problem?" Maya asked.

"Something is bothering you. You can tell us the problem and we will solve it." Greg assured.

"I think you missed something, Grandma," Lucinda said.

"What's that?" Maya asked.

"Lucinda, did you promise Maya that you would reunite her with Annalise? Annalise has been dead for eight years now. Don't make promises that can't be fulfilled." Greg chided.

"Was my mom born in this town," Lucinda asked as Maya and Greg looked at each other.

"Yes, but I didn't tell you that. How did you know?" Maya asked.

"That shouldn't be a problem. It all makes sense now. Why did you bring me here when you left this place and relocated to the village ***beyond the mountain ranges****?" Lucinda asked.*

"Because, we had issues and things were tight for us, we had to go back to the village a few months after your mom was born," Greg replied.

"Maybe you should have waited longer for the full blood moon. Maybe her death would have been averted," Lucinda said.

"What are you talking about?" Maya asked.

"I am trying to say that, I don't make promises that I can't fulfill. Nothing is impossible in my world because I rule in it. So, yes Grandpa, I promised Grandma that I would reunite her with her daughter. Just watch and see. It will all make sense someday. It's my promise to both of you," Lucinda said as she walked out and went into her room.

"What did you tell her?" Greg asked.

"I just told her the circumstances surrounding the birth of her mom, Annalise. She wanted to know, and I told her. But I never mentioned this town to her. I don't understand how she got to find out." Maya said.

"And she said something about the full blood moon and that nothing is impossible in her world," Greg asked, looking worried.

"Don't be word catch police Greg, we have just this world. Which another world can she be talking about?" Maya asked.

"I hope it makes sense someday. Just like she said, because I want to know why she said all these things," Greg said.

"Let me get your food," Maya said as she stood up and left the sitting room.

As the months rolled by, Greg and Maya tried to convince Lucinda to go outside and make friends, but their pleas fell on deaf ears. That wasn't what she was after. She was determined to set everything right and she was going to keep her promise.

"I think it's time. They deserve to know." Lucinda said as she looked out to see that the sky was covered with stars and a full moon.

"They agreed with me. They are solidly behind me," Lucinda said as she smiled and covered herself up as she drifted off to sleep.

◆ ◆ ◆

CHAPTER THREE

Lucinda knew it was time to meet her fellow goddesses, seek answers to her questions, and provide clues to her quest for a solution. She needed to find a way to do this and end her guilt. Her grandparents deserved the truth. After all, she surmised that Annalise and Phil were their children too.

Waking up in the morning, and after taking her bath and dressing up, Lucinda went straight to her grandparent's room. Greg, her grandpa, answered the knock on the door.

"Lucinda, you're up already and even dressed up too. Where are you going?" Greg asked.

"I will explain when I'm back. I just wanted to inform you that I'm going out," Lucinda said as she walked out of the house to the stable.

She untied the white horse's leash and mounted her. She was going back to the village where she was born. She wanted to ask questions and she was going to get it. It didn't take up to three hours before Lucinda arrived at her parents' house. She tied the horse to one of the house's pillars before walking inside.

As expected, everywhere was dusty, as it had been almost close to a decade that no one had lived there. Lucinda walked into her room and beheld the tiny bed that used to be her crib. She betrayed a wry smile, wavering her head in the process and muttering a little bit audibly, "Indeed, how time flies."

Standing at the doorway, she felt a sensation like she never experienced before. She quickly swallowed the saliva gathered in her mouth: reminiscing her childhood flooded her mind. She remembered the day she lost her parents. She remembered it as if it was yesterday.

Even though she could still get to see her parents, she wished they were alive, and if they were alive, she wouldn't have any reason to leave the village. She felt that unseen hands programmed the entire thing. Turning back, she walked out of the house and headed towards the river. She didn't want to enter her parents' bedroom.

When she got to the riverbank, she sat down there and threw pebbles into the river. She was there to find answers to her troubled mind.

"Mia, I know you can hear me, very loud and clear. I'm just here to ask questions, and I feel very strongly that you have the answers to my questions. My heart is heavy, and I have this burden on my shoulders that I need to lift. You've got to help me, Mia, please.

You, of all goddesses, need to help me. I need to bridge this gap between my dead parents and my grandparents. I know it can be done. I know that nothing is impossible." Lucinda said.

"You already have your parents back. What else do you want?" A voice sounded as Lucinda turned to see Mia at her back, about a few steps away.

Mia walked towards Lucinda with measured steps, in her full bloom, as her hair fluttered with the wind. On getting to where Lucinda sat on the river bed, she sat down but had her legs dipped into the river.

"I'm tired of living with the guilt of my grandparents not

knowing what is happening around them concerning their children, Annalise and Phil. I'm tired of hiding this.

I feel that my grandparents deserve to know the truth. After all, Annalise and Phil were their children, too. I have kept the secret for a long time because they don't understand what is happening. But I don't want it to be so anymore. I want them to see and hear their children again.

They deserve to know that their children still live though they are dead. I want them to have that same feeling of excitement in them, but I don't know how to make it happen. And please don't tell me you have no idea how to go about it because I know you do. I believe you can help me out." Lucinda said.

"That's the problem. I can't help you. You see these riddles you're trying to solve. You are the only one with the answers." Mia said.

"Why do you like giving me these blank answers each time I approach you? If I know the answer to the riddle I seek, do you think I will be here?" Lucinda asked, obviously frustrated.

"I don't even know how I'm not like you. Though you do not know it, I'm different. You're wiser and stronger than the two of us, making you the earth goddess. The answers you seek and the solutions lie within you." Mia said as she slowly turned into water and was gone.

Lucinda remained there speechless, angry, and sad at the same time.

"She didn't even give me a single clue to sorting out what borders my mind. Why do they keep telling me that I have the answers to all the questions I seek? Can't they see that I am human? If I have the answers, will I even ask anyone?" Lucinda said.

"It's not frustrating. It shouldn't be. That's the truth. The truth is that for some questions, you are the only one with the answers." A voice sounded nearby.

"Tara, is that you?" Lucinda asked, still having her gaze upon the water.

"Yes, it's me. I'm glad you're able to recognize my voice. Your tears drew me down to this place." Tara said, and that was when Lucinda realized she had been crying.

"I just want my grandparents to be able to see their children. That's all that I want. I want them to hear their voices again. I have been living with them ever since I lost my parents, and they have been the best grandparents ever. They haven't given me any reason to cry. My happiness is their utmost priority.

So, I think they deserve to know that their children still live even though they are dead. They also deserve to know who I am. They know that Lucinda is just their grandchild, but I think they deserve to know that I'm not fully mortal like them, that I'm something else, and that I'm the daughter of the moon and stars." Lucinda said.

"How I wish I have the answers to the questions you seek. How I wish I could make all that happen, but the truth is, I can't, but Bertha might know how you can go about it as she is the goddess of the wind. She is everywhere. She might have answers to that which you seek." Tara said.

"But Mia said I'm the only one who has the answers to the riddle." Lucinda offered.

"Yes, Bertha can only tell you the answers, but Bertha can't make them happen. You're the only one who can make it happen, and mind you, Bertha will give you a riddle to solve. It can know how to make your grandparents hear and see your parents again when solved." Tara replied. On hearing this, Lucinda was happy that at least there was hope.

"Even though I didn't find answers to my questions but then thanks to you and Mia, at least you both gave me a listening ear and offered me a line of hope," Lucinda said as she stood up and walked away. She turned to look and saw that Tara wasn't there anymore. She had disappeared just as she appeared.

****

When Lucinda got back, she took the horse into the stable and went inside the house.

"You're back, Lucinda. Watch the house. We want to get something at the market and be back in the next hour." Maya said from the window as soon as Lucinda entered through the back door.

"And when we are back, you have to explain where you went and why you have a frown on your face," Greg shouted.

Lucinda ignored them and turned back towards the garden. She was there all alone in silence. Soon after, she heard the door banging to know her grandparents were on their way out.

Lucinda sat there feeling dejected. She was worried that the promise she made to her grandparents might not be fulfilled after all, and she needed to keep to her promise. Her grandparents deserved to know the truth about her. Lucinda was racking her brain.

Suddenly Lucinda sensed a strong aura lurking around her. She knew someone was around.

"You are sad. You seek answers to your questions," a voice intoned. The voice was that of a whirlwind.

"Of course, I'm sad. I lived with my grandparents for eight good years and recently learned about my grandmother's pain and stigma before she had my mother. She was telling me the story herself. All I saw was a broken woman whose death cheated, a woman who fate mistreated, taking away her bundle of joy, a woman who never spent enough time with her child as my mom died when she was just 28 years old. Even though Granny is just trying to act strong and always smile, deep down her, I know the death of her child still hurts her today.

As she was telling her story, the story of her battle with childlessness, she tried so hard not to cry in my presence. *I promised her I would reunite her with her lost daughter, and she thinks I'm insane, but I still want to keep to that promise.*

I have had the opportunity to speak with my parents and even see them, and my grandparents know nothing about it. I think the little way of saying thank you for all these years is to give them the opportunity of seeing their children, Annalise and Phil.

But the problem remains how no one has the answers to my questions, not even Mia or Tara. I still believe that nothing is impossible in my world, but I can't yet understand why it looks as if it is impossible.

You all had lived in this world for thousands of years before I came into existence, so somehow any of you should have a hint on how to make my wish come to fruition. My grandparents deserve to know the truth and see their children again.

My grandmother needs her child, Annalise. When I look at my grandmother, I only see a woman who will give up the entire world for her child, someone who will trade her own life for her child. Please help me, help me put a smile on my grandparent's faces. Help me so I can say a proper thank you. Help me so I can reunite them with their children. That's all I ask for." Lucinda concluded as tears gushed freely from her eyes.

"The seashell holds the answer to the question which you seek. Mia said only you could solve the puzzle," Bertha replied after silently observing Lucinda for some minutes.

"The seashell? What do you mean? I know the seashell grants wishes, but I doubt it can make all these come through. How can the seashell help me out?

"The seashell will give you a link to make all of these come through. You have so many powers that you do not know of. But you need to know that no road on this earth is easy. Your road isn't easy, but they knew you were fit to solve all these mysteries when the crown was placed on your head." Bertha said.

"**The seashell**?" Lucinda muttered.

"I believe you can solve this puzzle. Have faith in yourself and see things work out right before your very eyes, the way you will never going to believe." Bertha said.

"But..." Lucinda turned to say something to Bertha, but she was nowhere to be seen. Having delivered her message, she has gone back to where she came from.

"Thank you, Bertha. I know you can hear me. I hope I will be able to sort this out." Lucinda said as she looked up at the sky where she sat in the garden.

Next, she stood up immediately and went inside her room. When she got there, she locked her doors, took out the seashell from where she hid it and placed her hand on it. She said, "I know you can hear me. They said you have the link to fix this puzzle, and once I fix it, I will be the happiest person on earth.

I should have done this since, but I feel this is the time to settle everything. Indeed, there is time for everything. Please help me, seashell. I need to reunite my grandparents with Annalise and Phil's children. You have got to help me.

Though she is acting all strong and fine, that woman has been bleeding over the death of her child. Fate has been unfair to her. Nature cheated her. Death won over her several times through several miscarriages. I just need answers on making my grandparents see and hear their children.

When I said nothing is impossible in my world, I meant it. Though I don't know, I know somehow answers will get to me. Could you help me fix this and reunite them? Tell me how I need to sort this out." Lucinda finished saying as she started crying. As she was crying, she was hoping for answers from the seashell. Lucinda waited patiently, but nothing happened. She was crying softly as her tears started dropping on the seashell.

"Bertha didn't lie to me. No one has the right to lie to the daughter of the moon and the stars. She wasn't lying when she asked me to come and meet you to answer my questions.

Why then are you keeping quiet? Why isn't anything happening? You all can't shut me out like this. I want to fix this problem, to bridge this gap. I can't do this on my own. I knew you all were sent to me because I believe you will have a part to play for my journey to be easier. So, why are you all silent?

Why won't you help? Why can't you tell me how to fix this? I need to reunite them, and I will, even if that's the last thing I will do on earth." Lucinda said as she dropped the seashell and lay on her bed, crying profusely.

"The wish; she has to make a wish on the night of the full blood moon." A voice whispered slowly and quietly.

"What wish? Who needs to make the wish?" Lucinda asked, but no one replied.

"The wish; she has to make a wish on the night of the full blood moon." The voice whispered slowly and quietly, again.

It was now left for Lucinda to figure out the rest. Time was of the essence as the blood moon would happen in less than a week.

Lucinda muttered, "Now I need to fix this, Clearing her eyes. What wish could this be, and who needs to make the wish?"

When she heard the front door opening, Lucinda lay on her bed thinking hard, trying to connect things to make sense. She knew her grandparents were back, and she knew that one of them would walk into her room in a few minutes.

And shortly after, Lucinda heard a knock on her door. It was a faint knock, but a knock always filled with tenderness and much love.

"Come in," Lucinda said.

Greg opened the door as he walked inside and sat on the edge of the bed.

"It seems something is troubling you. What's it?" Greg asked.

"I'm okay, Grandpa," Lucinda replied.

"But your face has given you away. It's written all over you. So what mystery are you trying to unravel this time around?" Greg asked as Lucinda sat up properly as a particular thought crept into her mind that perhaps her grandfather could be of help.

"Grandpa, can I ask you a question?" Lucinda said.

"Sure, I'm all ears. You can go ahead and ask me anything." Greg replied.

"When everything that concerns one revolves around a wish, including her birth, and to solve a problem, I mean bridge a gap, a wish has to be made, right? Who do you think should make the wish?" Lucinda asked.

"Lucinda, is this question about you? If yes, it's not going to work. Do you get it?" Greg replied.

"It's not about me, and if it's about me, why did you say it's not going to work? Maybe you should explain better." Lucinda.

"There is no need to explain since it isn't you," Greg said, standing up as Lucinda stood up too immediately and held her grandfather's hand.

"Please, Grandpa, I promise this will make sense someday. Just help me answer the puzzle, please. You don't know the weight of the burden you'll lift from my shoulders if you answer this question." Lucinda said, almost on the verge of tears.

"I said it won't work because the one who has to make the wish is gone. She has been gone for the past eight years, dead and buried, and I think you should forget about it. So, with that, I mean your mom, Annalise, but if it's someone else, her mother has to make the wish. So, the mother has to be the one whose wish can fix the gap." Greg said as he left the room.

Lucinda sat on the bed and placed her hand on her face, buried in deep thoughts.

"So, Mom has to make the wish? How can I even ask her to make a wish? She will know that I'm up to something. Can't I do this without involving her? Why does she have to be the one to make the wish?" Lucinda asked herself, pacing up about her room as the plot seemed dead on arrival. She just didn't know what to do. She knew there was no way her mom could make that wish without suspecting that she was up to something.

Lucinda ate her dinner that night and retired early to bed. When she woke up, it was already 1 am. Lucinda stood up and locked her door. Next, she held onto her necklace, closing her eyes;

and on opening it, she found herself on the bush path where she usually met with her parents, Amber and Anya. They were already sitting there in circles, waiting for her.

"I'm sorry I'm late. I was thinking about a few things, and I slept off, and when I woke up, it was already 1 am." Lucinda said as she sat down in their midst.

"Once again, something is bothering you. Do you mind sharing it?" Amber said.

"Nothing; I'm fine," Lucinda replied.

"You know we can always help when the need arises. Just tell us what the problem is, and we are ready to help." Phil chimed in.

"Lucinda, you're trying so hard to act fine, but it's written all over your face that something is wrong somewhere. I know you. I know the girl I gave birth to. I know when something is wrong with her." Annalise said.

"I feel she can sort it out. If she needs our help, she will speak up." Anya said.

"Anya is right. I can sort it out. There is nothing to worry about." Lucinda said.

"But I have a question to ask. Did Grandma tell you anything surrounding your birth?" Lucinda asked.

"No, because I didn't ask her as I felt it wasn't necessary, but what I know is that my mother was overprotective," Annalise said, smiling.

"Do you miss her? Have you ever wished that you could get to hold her and have a conversation with her?" Lucinda asked.

"Why do you ask?" Phil asked.

"Nothing really; just want to know," Lucinda said, smiling.

"Your grandmother is one of the best mothers-in-law. I see her as my mother. I was an orphan when I met your mom, and Maya proved to be the mother I didn't have all these years. So, yes, we miss her, but the truth remains that she can never see us or hear from us again. We are dead, and they are alive. There is a bridge between the dead and the living. You were able to break that barrier because of the powers bestowed on you," Phil said.

"I miss her. I do. She was my everything here on earth. I loved her the same way she loved me. Even though I asked her to give me siblings, she told me she was okay with just me. Of course, I miss her. There is no way I can deny that. I still want to have that conversation with her, hug her, and I will tell her how her smile is the most beautiful thing on earth. Those are mere imaginations that can't happen. As your dad said, there is a gap between the living and dead that is impossible to bridge." Annalise replied.

"What if nature decides to turn things around, and somehow you get to do all these things with your mother again. Will you reject it, or will you accept it wholeheartedly?" Lucinda asked.

◆ ◆ ◆

CHAPTER FOUR

Lucinda wanted more. She wouldn't accept having to wait only for midnights to see her parents, and even at that, once it was 3 am, they would have to part till another midnight?

She wouldn't accept the fact anymore of her grandparents not knowing about what was happening, of not being able to see their children and commune with them. Why wouldn't her grandparents be permitted to see, touch, and hear them?

It was becoming frustrating and even tasking, considering her having to come out most nights, enduring sleepless nights or half sleepless nights. Was she being selfish in demanding more? Wouldn't she have been contenting with the rare opportunity already granted her to see and hear her dead parents? She pondered these thoughts as she sat on her bed, getting ready to go out for the night as usual. As she was rummaging over these thoughts, she wavered her head in disagreement, insisting that she was not being selfish but only demanding what was the right thing to do under the circumstances. She wanted to start seeing her parents daily, in everyday interaction. Any other person out there would also have asked for the same thing. Which human being would be content with this unnatural arrangement?

These were her parents she lost when she was only a child, parents she never lived with for a long time, to savor the filial love and protection good parents give to their children.

Her joy in a child-parent relationship was short-lived and was cut short by their death. And now she knew she wanted them back at any price. She was determined to get them back to herself and her grandparents. She knew she could if she tried.

As the earth goddess and daughter of the moon and the stars, if she could not get whatever she wanted, who then should? Though her grandparents had tried their utmost to make her happy, the truth remained that the joy and bond of her parents were irreplaceable to her.

They were priceless. Still bearing these thoughts in her mind, Lucinda got up from the bed and stepped out of her room into the garden. When she got there, she down on the garden seat as she waited patiently for her grandparents to go out, and they just immediately notified her that they were leaving. She was excited. Once they were out of the house, Lucinda summoned Anya. She wanted to ask questions, and she hoped Anya would give her answers to her agitated mind.

"Surely something is bothering you that you couldn't wait till midnight?" Anya said as she appeared from nowhere.

"No, I can't wait, but you just scared me by your noiseless appearance." Lucinda half complained.

"You shouldn't be scared by that. Was it to be mere humans? I would understand, but not you. Anyway, sorry about that." Anya said as she sat down close to Lucinda. Lucinda couldn't help but admire the beautiful damsel sitting just close to her, yet she knew she was sitting close to a terrifying beast in her subconscious mind.

No one would believe that this pretty young girl sitting close to her was a deadly beast, not even Lucinda herself, as a mere mortal, would assume so. It surprised the thin line between Lucinda's natural world and humans. What appeared so fundamental to humans would not be what it was. But nothing could convince humans otherwise. They only could perceive through the five senses. Anything beyond that would be impossible to them.

"It's okay to admire my beauty, but I'm sure that's not why you summoned me. So, tell me, what's the problem?" Anya asked.

"My parents," Lucinda replied.

"What about your parents?" Anya asked.

"I'm tired of this midnight ritual of meeting them at a particular place, waiting for midnights every day before I can see them, and once it's 3 am, they are gone. I want to see them every day and restart a normal, natural relationship with them, just as we had before their death. I want to start interacting with them as naturally as I can be. Perhaps you might term me selfish, but I don't care. Besides, anyone out there would also ask for the same thing.

I know you can help me out, Anya. I want them to live with us here in this house, with you too. Please, I know you can make this happen." Lucinda pleaded.

"But have you thought about your grandparents and what their reaction could be? Would they ever be able to come to terms with that?" Anya asked.

"Don't worry about them; I will fix it," Lucinda said.

"Well, I can't make it happen. The only one who can do that is you. Only you can make that happen." Anya replied.

"But you are. "

"I'm Anya, the three-in-one being. I have been granted powers to do many things, but I can't promise you anything. I know that deep down, if you want this to work, you have to do it yourself. You have the powers to make it work. It's in you." Anya said.

"But how? I don't know. If I knew how I won't be asking you." Lucinda said.

"Maybe you don't know how but you have the powers to do it. You just have to go deep inside of you for the answers you seek." Anya said.

"Would Amber have an idea on how I'm going to go about it?" Digging inside wouldn't help me much, as I have done that severally without any answers. I need directions as I'm not wholly supernatural like you." Lucinda said.

"Amber won't answer the question. Listen, Lucinda, you are the daughter of the moon and the stars, and you have been bestowed with powers beyond what the mortal eyes can see, even beyond what you already know or can fathom.

You possess special powers that even you don't know. You ask questions that only you have answers to. The answer to the riddle that you seek lies in your palm. You can make it happen. You have to concentrate and figure it out, but whatever you do, make sure it won't ruin it for you in the future.

You have to be super careful because what you seek is quite extraordinary." Anya said as she stood up to leave.

"Where are you going? Lucinda protested. I'm not even finished with my questions."

"You're done with your questions, though you still have one question you can't ask me, and I don't even know what the question is. And secondly, your grandparents are on their way back so I should leave now. Check inside of your heart. Therein you will find answers to that which you seek." Anya replied as she went deeper into the garden, and just as Lucinda looked again, she was gone.

"Check inside of your heart. You will find answers to what you seek," Lucinda repeated the same thing Anya said.

"Why can't I just find the answers? Where else will I search? Why isn't my heart providing the answers that I seek? Why does everyone keep saying that I have answers to all I seek? Why?" Lucinda said, rubbing her forehead and racking her brain. She was beginning to feel frustrated.

Maya walked into the garden and sat close to Lucinda, but Lucinda didn't even notice that someone was sitting close to her until Maya tapped her, and she jerked.

"Hmmm. This is getting serious. You didn't even notice when I walked in?" Maya asked.

"Sorry, Grandma. I was lost in thoughts. You're back already. What about Grandpa?" Lucinda asked.

"Oh, he is inside, and we got something for you. Are you okay?" Maya asked.

"Yeah, can I ask a question?" Lucinda asked.

"Sure, why not."

"If you keep asking for answers to your questions and people keep telling you that you should look down inside your heart, that there you will find your answers, what does that mean?"

Lucinda asked.

"It means that the answers you seek are right there in your heart. You just need to sit and think, and it will reveal itself to you. ***Sometimes we search for solutions in the wrong places while the solution is right there.*** You will figure out all that you need to solve whatever it is." Maya said.

"Thank you, Grandma," Lucinda said with a smile.

"You're welcome," Maya said as she stood up and went inside.

"I need to bridge this gap that has been created by death, and also, I need to make my grandparents stay a little longer. Now, I'm faced with two tasks that I don't know which to do first, and I don't even know how to achieve them, not at all. I'm not selfish. I'm just being normal, natural. I'm not selfish to want my parents to stay for a long time without leaving once it's 3 am.

Any other person in my shoes will request for same. They were taken away from me when I was just ten years. Death separated us, and now that I can see and hear them again, it came with conditions.

Why are things way difficult when they should be made easy for me? Why do I have to go through so much to achieve so little? Life isn't fair.

I would be wicked if I said I needed to die to be with my parents completely. Doing so will be the same as killing my grandparents; their lives will be shattered and ruined. They will never forgive me. What do I do?

How do I fix this? How do I achieve all that I have mapped out? It's now looking impossible. I need help." Lucinda said in hushed tones with a teary voice.

She was tired. She was beginning to lose faith even in herself. Her level of frustration was increasing, and if not checked soon, she could reach the level of desperation and sadness. She had started feeling she couldn't endure it anymore, yet these immortals by her side expected her to be strong, but she wasn't sure of herself anymore. Even then, she didn't know how long she would take to achieve these things if they were ever to be completed.

As soon as Maya left, Lucinda also stood up as she went inside the house where she met her grandpa, who was resting with his eyes closed, obviously in thoughts.

Lucinda was almost at the door when she heard her grandfather's voice calling her. Getting closer to him, she answered.

"Sit down," Greg said as Lucinda sat down quietly.

"I know I haven't done anything wrong, or have I done something wrong?" Lucinda asked.

"No, you haven't done anything wrong, but I have been watching you for a few days now, and it's so obvious that something is eating you up. I know you will never answer me if I ask what the problem is, but that won't stop me from asking. So, what is the problem?

It hurts that you're fine this week, and the next week you carry a long face, and no one can be able to say what the problem is. We might not be able to bring back your dead parents, Lucinda. If we had the power to, we would have brought them back because we miss them too. Surely, you can't keep shutting us out like this. It's been eight years, Lucinda, yet you still haven't gotten over their death. One minute you're happy and looking all good, and the next minute my child is down with this sadness on her face. Where did we go wrong, Lucinda? Why is it difficult to accept the reality of death? Why can you not take us as your parents?" Greg asked, looking sad.

"I'm sorry, Grandpa if I have treated you and Grandma bad. I promise I didn't mean to. I never wanted it to be that way. I'm just trying to fix up things. I'm trying to patch up things so everyone will be happy.

I know I have been crisscrossing between two extremes of emotions, but I just can't help but know that soon, everything will be just where I want it to be. You and Grandma have tried to help me, and I appreciate it. I just want some more time to fix everything, and you all will understand what I have been going through for these past few years." Lucinda said while trying to manage a wry smile.

"How can we help if you don't tell us the problem? Why are you handling the problem alone when you know we might be of help to you?" Greg said.

"Grandpa, this is not as easy as you think. You and Grandma have already helped a lot, and this I must fix alone. No one can help me. I'm the only one who can help myself. I promise this will make sense to you and Grandma soon. Have faith in me." Lucinda pleaded.

"I hope I will be alive to witness that soon. I just hope, Lucinda. My health is waning bad, and I don't have much time. I don't know when my time will be up. We are all visitors here on earth, and when the time comes, we will leave." Greg said.

On hearing that, Lucinda rushed to where her grandpa was, and she hugged him tightly, whispering into his ears, "Nothing will happen to you. It's a promise. You will live for a long time, and when you get tired of living, you can go, but you aren't leaving us for now. About your health, you've healed already," Lucinda said with every seriousness.

"You're not a physician, Lucinda," Greg said.

"I'm not, but the powers and knowledge can't be compared to what I have," Lucinda said.

"And don't ask. I will explain all these when the time comes, but believe me when I said you're healed," Lucinda added as she smiled and went inside her room, leaving Greg confused about what she just said.

Lucinda got to her room, lay down on her bed, and soon immersed in her thoughts, soliloquizing. "How did I get so caught up with things that I didn't even notice my grandpa is slipping away?

How come I didn't notice how lean he has become? All I was after my happiness and to do things that would make me happy that I didn't even notice he had been sick all this while. What if he hadn't told me today? What would have happened?

At least I'm glad it's all over now. I made good use of my powers to heal my father, and all I can say is I'm proud of myself. I will do better this time. These two have sacrificed so much for me. I need to start paying attention to them and stop hiding in my room all day. I'm going to fix everything that soon they will meet Annalise and Phil.

Mom, I don't know how it will be, but you will make that wish." Lucinda said as she closed her eyes slowly and drifted off to sleep. All she knew was that things were going to be okay soon. She was so sure of that.

Lucinda counted the days and knew that the day of the blood moon was fast approaching. Though she saw her parents every night, that didn't erase her sadness.

Even when Lucinda tried to act all happy in the presence of her grandparents because she still had this sad smile on her face, she tried hard to conceal it. She didn't want anyone to know what she was going through. Nevertheless, Lucinda was optimistic that she would fix these and make everything possible.

As the days of the blood moon drew nearer, she started spending more time in the garden talking to herself. Whenever Maya and Greg tried to strike up a conversation with her, they would notice it wasn't flowing. They knew something was eating Lucinda up, but they didn't see the issue. All she thought about was how she could get her mom into making that wish because of the conversation she had with her these few days. It didn't seem like she was going to make any wishes again.

Lucinda was out to achieve two things. Though Anya knew the second one, she kept the first one a secret.

First, she contrived to trick her mother into making the wish—the wish needed to be made. Lucinda knew the desire was pivotal to the solution, the solution that would guarantee the happiness of everyone involved.

She just couldn't imagine the smiles on the faces of her grandparents when they would get to hear the voice of their children again.

The D-day came, and she had not yet achieved her aim of making her mom make the wish. So, she prayed instead that things change so the full blood moon won't come out that night, but she was disappointed to look up at the sky through her window to see the blood moon. She sighed and sat down on her bed.

Lucinda knew it was today or never if she had to succeed, facing her fate alone and with nothing to do about the situation. Otherwise, she would have to wait till the next year before she could do what she wanted, but she wasn't prepared to wait for that long. She needed to take action that night, hoping things would turn out well for her. As Lucinda sat on her bed brooding over the problem, she didn't know when it was just a few minutes before midnight. On noticing that, she stood up and locked her door while clutching her necklace. Next, she opened her eyes to see herself standing on the path she usually met with her parents. She sat there and waited patiently for them.

"This will be either a tough night or a smooth one. I don't know which one will be, but I want everything to be perfect. To the moon and the stars of the sky, I hope you can listen to your daughter.

I need your help this night. I want everything I planned to turn out well. *Help me to make my mom make the wish.* I need her to be able to speak with her mom again. Though my grandma acts all right, she is still in pain over her daughter's death.

You know it's the same daughter she begged for, the same

daughter she waited for ten years so she could have, the same child she cried to you. Now is the time to show that you can help me as I need your help to carry out this task. I know you can make this work. My mom must make the wish tonight. Please, listen to me and grant me this one wish. I beg of you." Lucinda said amidst tears.

And just when it struck midnight, Lucinda started hearing the howling of the wolves, an indication that Anya was about to appear. And soon after, Anya seemed to look completely emotionless, not happy, not sad, just plain. She came before Amber and Lucinda's parents got there later. They all sat down, and they started discussing in hushed tones, talking about the foibles of humans. Time was going so fast, and Lucinda didn't know how to bring up the discussion about her grandparents.

"The moon and the stars, help your daughter, I'm pleading. Don't forsake me now. I don't even know how to kick start my plans. I don't know." Lucinda muttered within herself, almost on the verge of tears.

"I miss my mom's stories. I don't go to bed any night without her telling me these beautiful stories. Even when I got married and visited, she would always tell me stories. I miss her." Annalise suddenly changed the topic of discussion.

Lucinda looked up as her face beamed with smiles, as this was something she was patiently waiting for.

"Does she tell you any stories?" Annalise asked, looking at Lucinda.

"Not really. Ever since you guys left, my relationship with my grandparents went from a hundred to zero. I always lock myself up in the room, though she listens and tells me if I ask her for stories. How I wish she could hear you, Mom, and also Dad. Maybe they won't have to see me as one who is going crazy anymore," Lucinda said.

"I have this feeling that someday they will be able to hear us," Phil said.

"*That's true. I just want to hear her stories again. I wish my mom and dad could hear me, and my husband. I wish they could hear us.*" Annalise's said as she slowly faded away.

Lucinda smiled, knowing her mom made the wish at the right time. Her face was filled with so much happiness. Anya looked at her and smiled before she changed and raced into the woods.

"I don't even know how I'm going to thank you. I don't even know where to start or what to say. Just when I thought all hope was lost, that I would have to wait till next year, you changed everything. I made my wish, and you made it happen. So, thank you! Thank you so much! I'm the happiest human on earth right now! The only thing I want has been accomplished." Lucinda said, smiling as she gathered herself up to leave too.

"I heard my daughter's wish, and I acted just like she wanted. You have been sad for years. If this is the only thing that can make you happy, I will do it for you. She took good care of my daughter, so they need to reunite with each other." An old-young voice said calmly to the hearing of Lucinda. It was the first time Lucinda heard this voice. It sounded like a mixture of light and darkness, thunder and lightning, the voice of a child and that of the aged.

"Thanks to the queen mother. I hope that one day I shall see you." Lucinda found herself saying.

"Not soon, but I will always be with you. ***Your job here on earth isn't finished. You can only see me when your work here is finished.*** " The voice said.

Lucinda smiled as she held her necklace, and immediately she was in her room. She quietly lay on the bed as she kept smiling.

She was so happy that she heard her voice for the first time, the voice of the one who owned her. It was the voice of the woman in whose loins she was formed and was given to her earthly mother to bear. She was so happy as she kept grinning from ear to ear.

"Lucinda, I'm happy that you're smiling right now. I don't know what you did, but whatever it was, I know it's for good since you're smiling; I love you, child." Again, it was Phil's voice.

"Goodnight, Dad," Lucinda said as she closed her eyes and drifted off to bed. She just couldn't wait for her grandparents to wake up.

◆ ◆ ◆

CHAPTER FIVE

Lucinda walked into the sitting room and quietly sat down, looking as if she wasn't in the mood to talk. After sitting down and not saying anything, her grandparents became uncomfortable with her moody stare. She sat down opposite them, with eyes filled with words and a silent mouth that remained sealed.

"Is everything okay?" Maya asked as she couldn't hold it anymore and was alarmed. Lucinda pretended as if she didn't hear her, but after another long stare at her and then at Greg, she calmly started talking: "There are two people so dear to you who wish to talk. You already know them, so there won't be any need for introduction." Lucinda said as a matter of fact.

"Talk to us? Who? From where? What are you talking about?" Greg asked, confused.

"You just walked out of your room alone. Who are those that want to talk to us? Besides, no one else is here except the three of us. So, what are you referring to, or are they standing outside?" Maya asked, looking confused.

"Mom, Dad!" The voice sounded.

"Can you hear us?" Phil's voice added.

"What's happening? Am I dreaming?" Maya asked, feeling so confused.

"It's Annalise and Phil's voice; Lucinda, what did you do?" Greg asked, feeling a swell of excitement in his bosom.

"She didn't do anything ill. All she wanted was for her grandparents to hear the voice of her children again." Phil's voice said.

"It's eight years now, and you can still remember our voice. I feel so happy that today you both can hear us." Annalise's voice added.

"Annalise, Phil, is that you?" Maya asked, almost on the verge of crying her eyes out.

"Yes, I'm the one, Mom." Annalise intoned.

"Someone, wake me up from this dream. This can't be real," Greg said.

"It's real. It's us. I hope somehow you will be able to see and feel us someday." Phil's said.

"***Okay, this was what I have been working on. Remember I once said it's all going to make sense someday. This is what I was talking about.*** I have been in touch with my parents for the past eight years, but the whole issue was that you both couldn't hear them. There wasn't any need to explain to you both because when I tried to, you and Grandma thought I was going insane. I have always wanted to fix this gap, and I'm glad I can do that, even if it's still partial."

"How is it possible? How did you manage to do all this?" Greg asked.

"The wish you made, Grandma," Lucinda replied.

"What wish are you talking about?" Maya said.

"Remember when you wished that the moon and the stars should bless you with a child, and they did. It turned out mother also made that same wish, but the truth is, you two considered it as mere wishes. ***This eighteen-year-old girl standing right in front of you is half-human and half-mortal.***

I am the daughter of the moon and stars, who have been bestowed with so many powers to do everything.

You and Mom's wish years ago made me who I am today. Though I didn't find it funny when I realized who I am, I had to accept it in good faith, and all I can say is that I'm happy my grandparents can hear their children's voice again after eight whole years." Lucinda said.

"I don't even know what to say," Maya said, sitting stuck on the chair as if glued to it.

"I will explain more tonight. Just wait," Lucinda said.

"This explains the howling of the wolves that I heard the night Annalise was born, right?" Greg said.

"*Exactly! The howling of wolves welcomes every daughter of the moon and the stars.* It is the same way they howled during my birth.

Your daughter, Annalise, is also a daughter of the moon and the stars, but the initiation wasn't complete because you took her out of this town and after she had me, fate brought us back here for me to pick up the crown that my mom wasn't able to wear. The universe was listening all these while weaving its ways around humans." Lucinda said.

"No wonder Annalise fell very ill after she left the town, and we thought she wasn't going to make it, but somehow she survived."

"That was when they called you to bring back their child because the place you made the wish has to be the same place where the initiation was completed. When my mom didn't return, I was brought here. I was born to replace my mom." Lucinda replied.

"Annalise! Phil!" Maya shouted in awe of what she was hearing.

"They won't hear you. they are gone, but you will hear from them soon," Lucinda assured as she went inside, but Greg was lost in thoughts.

"I see. All this while Lucinda was battling into accepting who she was. She couldn't tell us because we wouldn't understand.

So, Lucinda went on this journey alone for the past eight years. She was trying to fix the gap between us, desiring us to hear from them. Recently when I told her I was sick, she assured me I was healed, and up till today, there had been no sign of illness again.

She has been trying to fit into the life of mortals, trying to balance living with mortals with plenty of immortals by her side. It all makes sense now. I see." Greg reminisced, nodding.

"Lucinda, I'm very sorry," Maya said.

"Sorry about what, Grandma? Why are you apologizing? You don't have to, as you haven't done me any wrong." Lucinda sounded apologetic.

"I need to apologize. We didn't know you had been going through all these for eight years, trying to make us happy. Countless times you have given us hints of what you're going through, but what do we do? We continue feeling that it was the death of your parents that was affecting you, and because of that, we never paid attention to details that could have given a clue to what you were trying to do or who you are. We are sorry, Lucinda," Maya insisted.

"Yes, Lucinda, I feel the same way too. We are sorry and should have tried harder. We should have asked more questions." Greg said.

"No, you did. You did what good grandparents should have done in the circumstance. You were always concerned about me, but I kept it away from you all because I felt you were not going to believe me, and the truth was that there was no way you both would believe me if you couldn't have firsthand experience of whatever claim I would make.

Still, I knew someday things would change around. I only waited for the way you would hear them so I could explain everything that has been going on all these years.

Life has been fun and more fulfilling with you both, though sometimes I wish my parents never died. But then I would console myself with the fact that I got to hear their voices every night before eventually being able to start seeing them face to face.

I realized something the day I listened to your tale of how you had my mother. It was the same way you were hurt about her demise because of the constant pain, humiliation, and rejection you went through before you could give birth to her.

I knew I had to do something to reunite you all. I knew it was time to fill in the gap between you and them for eight years now. I started searching for ways. I asked the water goddess and fire goddess, but I got no concrete answers. When I asked the wind goddess, she gave me a clue. *And yes, the seashell you handed over to me so many years ago isn't just an ordinary seashell.*

It's a magical one, a priceless possession that can only work in the hands of the chosen one. I was able to find out that Mom had to make a wish for you to be able to hear for the gap to be closed. And somehow, she did because none of them knew what I was up to. I'm happy. I'm the most excited human on earth.

I got to reunite my grandparents with their dead children, as that has always been the task, and I'm glad I was able to put through it." Lucinda said, smiling as Greg and Maya walked closer to her and hugged her tightly.

"We are proud of you! Thank you so much for bringing them back. We can't see them, but at least hearing their voices again gladdens our heart." Greg said.

"We love you, Lucinda. Thank you for this." Maya said as tears dripped down her cheeks as Lucinda wiped them off with her hands.

"You shouldn't be crying, Grandma. Things are okay now. Don't worry. Everything will be complete soon." Lucinda said.

"But everything is completed already. We can hear them. What more can you do?" Greg asked.

Lucinda stepped back as she lifted her hands, and just with a snap of the finger, a ball of fire was sitting on her palm.

"Lucinda!" Maya shouted, shocked.

"You're going to get hurt!" Greg joined as Lucinda disappeared and appeared at his back.

Greg and Maya were shocked beyond words. "Who are you?" Lucinda.

"I'm still Lucinda, your granddaughter you have raised for eight years.

You know me as Lucinda but not as the daughter of the moon and the stars. I'm different, Grandpa; I'm entirely different. I possess supernatural powers, some of which I don't know. I'm not completely human. I'm Lucinda, but I'm immortal. That's who this girl is. Just wait, and you will see what will happen sooner." Lucinda smiled and walked inside her room, leaving her grandparents speechless.

"I guess we are in for a lot of surprises. She was either in her room or the garden. She must have been feeling lonely and sad all this while. It must have taken a whole time for her to accept who she is.

I know Lucinda to be a stubborn but sweet girl as well. I'm proud of her. I'm happy that she could pull through and how she has accepted who she is. I'm happy this new self-discovery didn't mar her. She acted wisely the same way Annalise would have acted. I couldn't have asked God for a better gift. I'm happy we have Lucinda here." Greg said, smiling contentedly.

"I'm happy she reunited me with my dead daughter and son-in-law. I don't know what to give her to thank you or appreciate her for what she did. Just when I got tired of questioning the universe on why they took Annalise from me.

Then Lucinda made it possible for us to communicate with them. Lucinda, in generations to come, your kids, strangers, and people from far and wide will bow at your feet and make you happy. You won't have any reason to cry in life. I hope all you wish for is granted unto you." Maya said, smiling as she hugged her husband.

Lucinda on bed staring at the ceiling. She was happy with herself. She was proud of herself, and best of all, she felt at peace with herself. She had just one thing left to do. She needed to behold the face of the woman whose loins she came out from.

She would see the queen of the moon and the stars. She had to meet her and thank her for blessing her with her earthly parents. Her parents and grandparents were the real deal, and she was grateful. She couldn't have asked for more.

"I guess that's why you pushed me into making the wish. I'm glad I listened to you. I could see the excitement and happiness in their faces when they heard our voices." It was Phil.

"I couldn't tell you and Dad what I'm up to. I wanted it to be a surprise. And after I listened to Grandma's tale of what she went through before she gave birth to you, I knew the only way I could make her happy was by reuniting the both of you."

She knew they were gone when she didn't hear their voice anymore. She then closed her eyes and drifted off to sleep.

◆ ◆ ◆

CHAPTER SIX

In the evening, Lucinda decided to take a stroll into the town and no sooner had she opened the door then Maya wanted to know where she was going.

"To look at the environment. I'll be back before 6 pm." Lucinda promised as she left the house, leaving Maya staring at her from behind.

When she got into the heart of the town, she went to a park with concrete seats scattered all over the place. She sat down, looking around her, and she couldn't help but admire the serene environment before her. It had been a long time since she visited the town. Most of these times of her troubles, she had always been inside or in the garden. Mingling with people inside the city reminded her of her humanity, though she didn't have any human friends.

As she sat down inside the park, she couldn't help but admire a little girl who held tightly onto her mom. Lucinda smiled and muttered, "She is beautiful." The little girl and her mom were taking a walk on the street. Lucinda decided to also take a walk all by herself.

As she went into the street, she suddenly felt a hard nudge on her body, and on turning around, she saw a young boy, slightly older than her, having his baskets and their contents on the ground, littering everywhere. She had pushed the boy without noticing it, as all her attention was on the people around her.

"I'm sorry. I didn't mean to. I just wasn't looking." Lucinda apologized as she helped and picked up the vegetables littered on the ground.

"It's okay," the boy said as he clutched tightly to his basket.

On looking at him, Lucinda felt something strange and unique, perhaps. His skin was white and his hair golden, like his eyeballs. His aura was so strong. Lucinda felt it.

"I'm Lucinda; who are you?" Lucinda said, trying to strike a conversation.

"I'm Jake. Next time, you have to be more careful," Jake said as he hurriedly walked off.

"Something was so strange about him," Lucinda muttered as she looked at him until he faded out of sight. "Who is he?" Why did I feel slight pain when my hand brushed his hands?" Lucinda muttered again but, finding no answers to her questions, had to turn and stroll back home, with the thought of Jake occupying her mind. She went through the back door into the sitting room when she got home, where she saw her grandparents. She just sat down beside her grandmother but looked moody.

"What's the problem? I can see that something is bothering you." Greg said.

"I saw someone today who looked different. His skin shone bright like the sun, and his hair and eyes were pure gold. He said his name was Jake. I want to find out more about him. Something is off somewhere about him. That's it. Nothing much." Lucinda said.

"Are you suggesting he is a bad person?" Maya asked.

"No; far from that, rather, he is good, but I want to know who and why he is here. He doesn't belong here. Something is so different, but I can't place my hand on it, and I need to find out why." Lucinda said.

"Do you like him?" Greg asked, looking at his granddaughter closely.

"What! No, not that." Lucinda stammered, blushing in the process.

"It's just that he looked different, and his aura is so strong, and I want to know more about him," Lucinda replied.

"Lucinda," Greg said, smiling.

"What's the problem, Grandpa?" Lucinda asked.

"Ever since we moved into this place, you haven't had someone to call a friend. You have been alone. Either you're inside your room or inside the garden and..."

"I have friends, Grandpa," Lucinda said, cutting her grandfather short.

"I don't mean your friends who aren't humans. I mean friends who are humans like us. Having one human friend won't hurt. If you like Jake, I hope fate brings you to see each other again. At least, that way, I can say my granddaughter has a friend whom she can talk to any time, any day." Greg said.

"Your grandfather is right, Lucinda. A time comes when we will not be here for you. We won't be with you forever, and you will be spending more years here on earth when we are gone. So, you have to get used to that fact. You need someone with whom you can talk, laugh, build memories, and do many other things." Maya said.

"Well, if I'm bored, I can always talk to you both. You both make me happy. Why then, do I need a friend?" Lucinda asked.

"You need a friend, a human friend. You have to start accepting that we won't be with you forever. We are aging beautifully, and soon, we will kiss goodbye to this earth." Greg said.

Lucinda thought of what she heard and decided to go inside her room. Once inside, she concluded that her grandparents were right.

"But how is that even possible when I barely know anyone? The worst thing is that I don't even know how to make friends. I have lived in this town for some years now, yet I do not know anyone or anywhere I can visit to make friends." She was muttering as she lay on her hand, looking up to the ceiling. She was gradually becoming restless.

Next, she stood up and walked out of the garden toward her room. She kept thinking about the boy amid a potpourri of other issues bothering her. But she couldn't seem to get her mind off the boy. She knew that something was special about him, but she couldn't get to know what at the moment.

On realizing her state of mind, she wanted answers and needed to talk to someone. She closed her eyes and mumbled some words. As she opened her eyes, Anya was sitting close to her.

"You summoned me. Hope there is no problem?" Anya asked as she sat near Lucinda.

"I need your help, Anya." Lucinda pleaded.

"Okay, you can tell me what the problem is," Anya said.

"I don't have friends. I don't mean to say you're not my friend. You're my friend, but I mean like human friends. Does that make me awkward? I mean, I'm eighteen, and in a few months, I will be nineteen, and I can't even boast of having any single friend. It has always been you and Amber, my parents, and my grandparents. I need to have, even if it's one human friend." Lucinda said.

"Let me guess; something happened today. Tell me about it." Anya said, smiling.

"Who are you talking to, Lucinda?" Maya said as she walked towards the garden.

"She can't see me, so it's no use explaining to her. Just come up with any good excuse." Anya said.

"Grandma, I'm just thinking out loud. You know, thinking about life," Lucinda said, faking a smile.

"Okay, no problem. Dinner will soon be ready. So, make sure you come in very soon." Maya said as she looked at her granddaughter one more time before leaving.

"How come she can't see you?" Lucinda asked.

"Because she isn't meant to see me. So, back to the main reason why you called me here. What happened?" Anya asked.

"I saw this boy today while strolling on the streets, and something seems odd about him. His eyes are pure gold, and his aura is so strong. He said his name is Jake," Lucinda said.

"His eyes are like pure gold, and yours is like that of the sky," Anya said, laughing.

"Anya, I'm serious," Lucinda said.

"Okay, you already know his name, so why did you call me here? I'm still trying to understand why you called me and what you need my help with." Anya said.

"I need to find Jake. I want to know where he lives, his parents, and where he is from. I want to know everything about him." Lucinda said.

"Why are you interested in someone you met today, and why do you want to know more about him? Have you fallen in love with him?" Anya asked.

"No! I just want to know. I have questions, and don't ask me what I intend to ask him." Lucinda said, smiling.

"Okay, I can't help you then," Anya said.

"Why?" Lucinda asked.

"Because no human fits into that description. So, most likely must have seen a spirit who came to the market to get some things. My dear Lucinda, the sooner you erase the thought of Jake or whatever his name is, the better for you. The person you saw isn't human." Anya said.

"No, he is human. Our bodies brushed against each other. You have to believe me, Anya." Lucinda pleaded.

"I believe you, but the truth is that he isn't human. His eyes are like pure gold. That sentence alone proves he isn't human like you. So, give up. You can't find him, and I can't find him too. And you made mention of friends. How did friends and this Jake relate to each other?" Anya asked.

"Ooh, you didn't get the connection? I'm looking to make him my human friend. I don't know, but my spirit accepted him. That's why I called you so you can find out everything about him." Lucinda said sadly.

"Aside from being the daughter of the moon and the stars, there are still things that you don't know. Don't worry. Soon, you will get to understand everything. It's just a matter of time." Anya said.

"I'm sure he is human. He is human." Lucinda insisted as she stood up and walked out of the garden.

"Jake met a goddess here today. What is he doing here? Why does it have to be Lucinda? I have to meet him." Anya said as she slowly faded away.

On leaving the garden, Lucinda sat on the sofa on the balcony. She just couldn't understand what Anya said to her that Jake wasn't human that made her so sad? As she was crying, she noticed someone standing next to her, wiping away her tears, and looked up to see that it was Jake. Lucinda looked at the figure to ensure the person was standing there. Lucinda was surprised.

"What are you doing here?" Lucinda asked Jake.

"I was on my way home when I saw you sitting here crying. Is there any problem?" Jake asked.

"No, there is no problem," Lucinda replied. Just then, Maya walked out to see Lucinda and Jake standing together.

"Lucinda, who is he?" Maya said, smiling.

"I'm Jake," he replied with a broad smile, without waiting for Lucinda to answer.

"I'm Maya, her grandmother. I guess you were the one who she met a few hours ago. She was right when she said your eyes are like pure gold." Maya said, smiling.

"Thank you," Jake replied, smiling.

"Is it okay to visit some other time? It's been some years since we moved in here, and this is the first time someone is coming to visit Lucinda. She will make a great friend." Maya offered.

"Granny!" Lucinda shrieked in awe of Maya's attitude.

"I'm her friend already. I will visit some other time." Jake replied.

"Nice. Lucinda's dinner is ready. Come inside and have something to eat." Maya said as she smiled and walked inside. Jake looked at Lucinda and smiled as he turned to leave, but Lucinda called him back.

"Your eyes, they are like that of pure gold. Who are you? Are you human?" Lucinda asked.

"And your eyes are like that of the sky. I'm Jake, and I'm just like you." Jake said as he walked away.

Lucinda stood there with her jaw dropped as she resolved to unravel the mystery called Jake fading away before her.

"What is happening to me?" Lucinda asked as she stood up and walked inside.

****

Jake was feeding the horse when he heard a noise at his back, but he continued with what he was doing as if he heard nothing.

"Why did you come to earth? Why did you choose Lucinda?" the voice asked.

"Our destinies were already fixed with each other even before she was born. Guess you told her that I'm not human. Anya, I'm a god, born to human parents. I'm still human." Jake replied as he turned to face Anya.

"Hurt her, and you will cease to exist, both human and god," Anya warned.

"I have no intention of hurting her as she is part of me. In a few months, she will be nineteen, and hope you're preparing her to meet the woman from whose loins she came out?" Jake asked.

"That isn't any of your business, Jake," Anya said. "The sooner my father and the queen of the moon and the stars end their quarrel, the better for you all. None of you can prevent this from happening. By the time she turns twenty, it will all make sense to her, and everything will be explicit." Jake said as he picked up the bucket on the ground by his side, ready to leave.

"Do they even know who you are?" Anya asked.

"Yes, they do. They found out the very day I was born on this earth. Anya, I know you're trying to protect Lucinda, and I appreciate all you have done, but you should understand that I have no intention of hurting Lucinda. I had to meet her today because she deserves to know who I am." Jake said and left, but halfway had to stop at the door as he turned to Anya and said: "Lucinda is wonderful."

He smiled as he walked out of the stable. Anya gnashed her teeth in anger.

"I hate his guts." She said as she disappeared from the stable.

◆ ◆ ◆

CHAPTER SEVEN

Lucinda ate quietly with her family that evening as her grandparents talked about many things, a potpourri of issues, reminiscing primarily on their past. As Lucinda listened to them, she was prompted to come in between their conversation.

"I want to say something," Lucinda said, looking at them.

"Okay, go ahead," Greg said.

"Is it possible to stay awake till midnight today, just for me? I want to take you both somewhere." Lucinda said.

"2 am? That's deep into the night. Where will you be taking us in the middle of the night? Lucinda, what are you planning?" Maya asked.

"No, you both aren't going to get hurt. I promise," Lucinda replied.

"Alright, we will stay awake just for you," Greg assured.

"Oh, my. Thank you so much," Lucinda said, smiling. She had earlier thought it would be difficult convincing her grandparents to stay awake. She knew they would be excited once they saw what she had in store.

Soon they finished up their dinner as Lucinda cleared the plates and walked straight to the kitchen to wash them. She walked back into the sitting room and joined her grandparents when she finished up.

She knew she had to engage them in a conversation to keep them awake, or they could fall asleep right there on the chair.

"So, tell me, Grandpa, do you think you will ever see Mom and Dad again?" Lucinda began.

"Sure, I will see them again. You know, no one lives forever. We all will die someday to start the journey to the world beyond. I will meet them; sure, I will," Greg said, smiling.

"What if they appear right now? What if it happens while you're still alive?" Lucinda asked.

"That can't be possible, can it?" Greg asked, looking perplexed.

"Well, with the universe, all things are possible. If the universe makes it possible, I will be the happiest human. To see my daughter's face again while I'm alive would be the greatest feeling for sure. I'm getting old, and the only thing that keeps me going is your face, Lucinda's because you look just like Annalise. Though it isn't possible to see the dead again, I know miracles happen." Maya said, smiling.

"Yea, miracles happen. Impossibilities are made possible. You just have to believe and watch how things will unfold." Lucinda assured.

"Thanks, my lovely angel," Maya said, grinning.

Greg smiled too. He knew his wife was ready to lay down her life just for Annalise to come back to life. She practically begged for a child, and when Annalise came, she became her whole world. It was so saddening to hear that fate took her away so soon.

They kept discussing, and when it struck midnight, Lucinda looked at her grandparents and asked, "Are you already?"

"Ready for what exactly," Greg asked, a bit irritated.

"Just give me a few minutes," Lucinda said as she walked into her room and returned a few minutes later. She instructed her grandparents to hold each other while placing one of her hands on her grandparent's entangled hands. She then touched her necklace, and in no time, they were standing at the pathway filled with bushes, her usual place of meeting with her parents and others.

"Wait. What are we doing here? How did it happen?" Maya asked.

"Where are we? Lucinda, what did you do? This is not even time for questions. We just have to leave here immediately. This place is dangerous. It's not safe for us to be out here inside the bush at this time. Let's go home, Lucinda," Greg said.

"Watch," Lucinda said as she pointed at the people sitting down close to a fire.

"Who are they?" Maya asked, casting a cursory glance at them.

"Before I answer that, let me tell you this. Ever since I asked you all to leave the town a few days after moving in, I spent my nights here after the monster saga. By midnight I come here and spend time with these beautiful people and by 3 am, I'm back home. They are the sole reason your granddaughter is still sane," Lucinda said.

"You haven't been sleeping at home all this time?" Maya asked, mouth agape.

"Yes, because I spend my night here. Let's move closer and see who they are." Lucinda said.

Lucinda shouted, "Annalise and Phil, look over here as they inched closer to people." They both looked up to see Lucinda standing with their parents after hearing Lucinda's voice.

"Annalise and Phil, is that you?" Greg asked as he came even closer.

"Yes, but how is this possible? How can you see us?" Phil said as he stood up with Annalise.

"Mom, can you see me?" Annalise asked Maya, looking at her with bated hope.

"You both can hug each other if you want," Lucinda said as Maya ran straight into her daughter's outstretched arms and hugged her tightly.

"It's been eight whole years, Annalise. I never thought I would see your face again," Maya said, crying.

Lucinda watched as Greg hugged Phil tightly. She left them and sat close to Anya and Amber, who watched as the four of them hugged each other without trying to let go.

"This was what you always wanted, right?" Anya asked, grinning.

"Yes, and I'm happy, but just one thing remaining, and I'm good to go," Lucinda said, smiling.

"Don't worry, the last one won't be difficult to achieve," Amber assured, smiling as Lucinda threw her hands on Anya and

Amber, hugging them tightly.

When Lucinda saw that her parents and grandparents were sitting, chitchatting, she looked at them and said, "So this is where I wanted to take you both. That's why I was asking those questions. This is Anya, the three in one beast, Amber." She introduced, widely grinning.

"Three in one beast? How do you mean?" Greg asked.

"When the city was being terrorized, and drops of blood were everywhere, she was the one doing that. I will go into details later and explain her reason for doing so, but she was sent for me to realize who I was. Aside from being human, she is a wolf and a shape-shifter. I mean, not just one. They are three when I say wolf. That's why she is called a three-in-one beast." Lucinda offered.

"She is so beautiful. She doesn't look like a beast or someone who can hurt someone." Maya enthused.

Anya smiled as she said, "Don't look at the face. I'm everything she said that I am."

"Amber, the seer," Lucinda said, turning to Amber.

"You have always wanted to see me ask questions, but you have not been able to. You wanted answers to many questions. She has already had her purpose, having traced her root, knowing who she is." Amber said.

"I never believed that I would be able to see you," Greg said.

"If Annalise and Phil are dead, Amber and Anya are dead too, right?" Maya asked, still trying to collect what was unfolding before them.

"Not really; Anya isn't fully human like us. Anya is from the other world, and Amber, I won't say she is dead." Lucinda replied.

"Oh, now I understand," Greg said as they sat around the fire.

"How did you do this?" Phil found himself asking finally.

"Let's say that nothing is impossible," Lucinda replied, smiling at her father.

Lucinda sat down near Anya and watched as they got along, chitchatting excitedly. Seeing the smiles on their faces, she was elated. This was what Lucinda had been dying to see, to see them meet together like this. She excused herself as she walked out of their presence, walking a bit far from them as she sat on the floor and looked up.

The moon was complete as the stars filled up the sky. She smiled and said, "I know you can hear me. I hope you're well. I know somehow I will be able to meet you someday and say thank you for everything you have done so far."

"You are my daughter. Your happiness is my happiness. I just want you to be happy," the mature voice answered.

"I want to request one more thing from you. I'm tired of coming here every night. Why do I have to wait every midnight before seeing my parents? It doesn't make sense to me. I deny myself sleep every day, and now that my grandparents are aware that they can't stay up every day because they are old.

I wish something would be done. I know I have made a lot of requests. I have asked for too many things, but I'm sorry. You know, death took my parents when I was just ten. They left too early. I didn't get to spend enough time with them. I wish their ghost would be living in our house, and we will see them every minute, living a normal human life," Lucinda said.

"But only on one condition," the voice said.

"From midnight, you will get to touch them and hug them, but once the clock strike 7 am, you can only see and hear from them, but you won't be able to touch them," the voice said.

"It's magnificent with me," Lucinda said, smiling, accompanied by flashes of lightning.

"I hope I will get to say a proper thank you one day," Lucinda said as she stood up and walked out of the bushes to go and meet the others.

"Where have you been, Lucinda?" Maya asked.

"It's night. You could get bitten by a snake. Are you're okay?" Greg asked.

"I'm okay. I just went to fix some things right. We need to get going so you can sleep." Lucinda said. Maya stood up, hugging Annalise and Phil tightly.

"I wish I could get to see you again and again," Maya said, almost on the verge of tears.

"You will. It's a promise," Lucinda said.

Greg hugged Annalise and Phil before Lucinda hugged them. She then waved at Anya and Amber before she held her grandparent's hands, and they disappeared out of sight. Lucinda hugged them and asked them to go to bed when they got home.

"Lucinda," Maya called as soon as Lucinda turned to walk out.

"Yes," Lucinda answered as she turned, looking at Maya.

"Thank you, darling. You don't know what you have done for me. Thank you so much." Maya said.

"We hope your children and grandchildren and great-grandchildren make you happy just like you have made us happy," Greg said.

"Thank you," Lucinda said as she smiled and walked into her room. Her body touched the bed no sooner than she drifted off to sleep.

In the morning, Lucinda woke up and had her bath. She walked out to meet her grandparents, who were already up and chatting with excitement.

"Grandpa, Grandma, I have something to show you," Lucinda said.

"Hmm. Another surprise? I hope you slept well? And you're up so early today. Well, what's that?" Maya asked.

"This," Lucinda said as she shifted from the door, and Greg and Maya were surprised to see Annalise and Phil standing there. Maya stood up immediately to hug them, but she found out she had gone through them.

"What's happening?" Maya said.

"You can only touch them from midnight to 7 am, but once it strikes 7 am, they go back to being ghosts. I had to make them come here. I just want you both to wake up and see your children.

You miss them. Even though you try so much to hide the hurt and anger, it's still visible for all to see. You need your children. Remember what you said at night. You wish you could see them again. I promised you that you would see them, and here they are," Lucinda said as Maya and Greg hugged her tightly.

"I don't know what we would have done without you. Thank you so much for everything, Lucinda. Thank you for making us this happy. We don't even know how to repay you." They both chorused.

"You don't need to repay me. You have been with me ever since they ceased being humans," Lucinda said.

"Does that mean you can see me, Annalise, and Phil?" Maya asked.

"Yes, Mom, we can," Annalise said.

"Everything. We can see everything," Phil said.

"I missed you both. For once, I thought I would never see you again after last night, but here you both are. Thank you," Maya said.

And as soon the words left Maya's mouth, Lucinda heard a knock on the door. She turned and opened it and was shocked to see who it was.

"Anya!!!" She shouted.

"The queen asked me to come. You need to be protected," Anya said as she walked into the house.

Lucinda closed the door as she dragged Anya to her room.

"Let me guess. This is what you went to the bush to consult the queen. I can see that your earthly parents treated you right, the reason you shower them with so much love." Anya said.

"If there were other words bigger than love, I would use that. Without them, then there is no Lucinda." Lucinda replied.

****

"Hey, look, Anya, that's Jake, the one I have been telling you about. Wait, let him come closer, then you look at his eyes." Lucinda said as soon as he saw Jake.

She had decided to take a stroll with Anya because she was bored at home. She wanted to interact more with humans and learn about their lives and everything that needed to be discovered.

She wanted her grandparents and her parents to spend enough time together, and at this moment, what she wanted more was just human friends. She wasn't getting younger. She was getting older, and she still needed human friends around her irrespective of being immortal, even if it was just one.

She waved at him as Jake walked closer to where she was standing with Anya.

"What are you doing here?" Jake asked.

"I felt bored at home, and I decided to come out with my friend. Her name is Anya," Lucinda replied.

"Oh, what about your parents and also your grandparents? Aren't they keeping you company?" Jake said, avoiding contact with Anya.

"About that; my parents died eight years ago, and I live with my grandparents," Lucinda said.

"Oh, I'm so sorry about that," Jake said, turning to Anya. He said, "And Anya, my name is Jake, Lucinda's friend," Jake said, stretching his hand for a handshake.

Anya looked at him and said to Lucinda without taking his hand, "I will be waiting for you at the tree close to the house; I will leave you two to talk to each other." Anya said as she left them to be alone.

"I'm sorry; she isn't comfortable with strangers." Lucinda apologized, feeling sad over the way Anya treated Jake.

"That's not an issue; I understand," Jake replied.

"What are you doing here? You came all alone?" Lucinda asked.

"Oh yes, I went to the market to get vegetables to make soup. As you can see, I'm on my way home," Jake replied.

"Oh, that's nice. Guess your mom is going to prepare that?" Lucinda asked.

"No, my parents have passed away. I will prepare this myself, and just so you know, I'm not a baby like you. I'm twenty-three years. I'm older than you." Jake said.

"Yeah, sure, but that doesn't matter. I'm sorry about your parents." Lucinda replied.

"Yeah, sure, it doesn't matter. I need to get going. Your friend must be waiting for you. It would be best if you didn't keep her waiting; and my parents, it's okay. It's been five years without them, and I'm adapting." Jake replied.

"Yeah, true," Lucinda said as she smiled dryly.

And without warning, Jake came closer and hugged her before leaving. Lucinda was shocked as she tried to figure out what had just happened.

"Did he just hug me, just like that?" Lucinda asked herself.

She smiled as she walked home, grinning. She loved the feeling. Along the way, she spotted Anya waiting for her at the tree just as she promised.

"You don't like Jake," Lucinda said as soon as she got close to Anya.

"Why did you say so? I don't hate him." Anya said.

"But you refused to take his hand when he offered a handshake. Is everything okay?" Lucinda asked.

"That doesn't mean I hate him, and yes, everything is okay. Why did you ask?" Anya asked.

"Because I saw how you looked at him with so much contempt and disgust. You barely know him, and you mistreated him. Remember you even said no human fits my description of him? You can now see that he is real." Lucinda quipped.

"Yeah, but the question is, is he human? Let's go home, Lucinda," Anya said.

Lucinda followed suit, pondering what Anya said about Jake not being human. Lucinda tried so many times to make Anya explain what she meant by that, but Anya remained mute. Lucinda then swore that she would find out the truth and that not even anyone could stop her.

When Lucinda found out her grandparents were still asleep, she left the bedroom the following day. As she tried walking out of the house, she heard her mom's voice.

"Where are you going? Isn't it early?" Annalise asked.

"I will be home soon. When Grandpa and Grandma wake up, tell them I went out to get something." Lucinda said and dashed out of the house.

Lucinda didn't wait to hear her mom's response or what her father would have to say. Living with her parent's spirits and seeing them every day gladdens her heart. She never for once thought that a day like this would ever come.

Lucinda strolled towards the other street. She felt that finding Jake's house won't be difficult for her, as she knew how to use her powers.

Soon she was able to identify the house. When she got to the house, she stood at the door and knocked severally; and just when the door opened, Jake was shocked to see her standing there.

"What are you doing here, and how did you find out where I live?" Jake asked.

"I'm not desperate. I'm only here to ask you a question," Lucinda said.

"Questions?" Jake said as he opened the door wider for Lucinda to come in.

"No, that won't be necessary. I'd rather sit here on the balcony and ask you what I want." Lucinda said.

Jake looked at her awkwardly as he came out and sat on the rocking chair on the balcony while Lucinda leaned against the rail.

"I'm all ears. So, what is this that you wanted to ask me that you couldn't wait, and how did you even get to know where I live?" Jake asked, still surprised.

"Finding out where you live isn't difficult for me," Lucinda replied.

"Maybe you can explain," Jake said.

"I will explain all that later, but not today. So, tell me, are you human?" Lucinda asked pointedly in her usual way.

Jake looked at her. His jaw dropped as if she had dropped a bomb. "Who knows what Anya must have told her. What is she trying to do? Anya is simply making things difficult for me. She is trying to ruin everything because she is Lucinda's guardian." Jake silently reasoned.

Lucinda waited for the answer to come from Jake, but it was taking more time than necessary, which made her suspicious.

"So, does that mean what she said is true?" Lucinda asked.

"Wait! Seriously, who is feeding you with all these? Why will you even ask if I'm human? Don't I have the same features as humans? And who even suggested that to you?" Jake said, acting upset.

"You don't need to be upset; you just have to answer the question," Lucinda said.

"I'm human, and well, if anyone tells you I'm not human, then it's obvious the person isn't human too, because it takes a nonhuman to know one who is a human and one who is not. Yes, I'm a human. I am. But why would she even insinuate such about me that I'm not human?" Jake asked.

"Your features do not fit into typical humans. Your eyes are nothing but pure gold," Lucinda said, eyeing him.

"That's because I'm different. I have always been different. I'm human, just like you. I know it's strange for a human to be blessed with eyes of gold but let's say nature has its way of blessing people, and I'm a blessing to my late parents." Jake reiterated.

Lucinda tried touching Jake's forehead, but Jake held her hand before it could get to his forehead.

"What are you doing?" Jake protested as he held Lucinda's hand.

"I wanted to check something. This mark on your forehead that looks golden too," Lucinda said.

Jake knew there was no way he would allow Lucinda to touch his forehead because once she did that, she would fully understand that he wasn't human. She wasn't human too, but some things were better left hidden.

"That's a birthmark. You need to go now. Your grandparents will be worried sick if they find out you're not at home." Jake said as he dropped Lucinda's hand and hugged her abruptly once again while whispering, "I'm a human, Lucinda." standing up, she walked inside.

Lucinda smiled as she stood up and strolled back home.

Jake opened the door to see Anya sitting comfortably on the chair. Jake sat on the other chair and looked at her without uttering. But after a minutes of silence, he started talking.

"Why are you doing this? Why are you making this difficult for me? If the two supreme beings have issues, don't drag me into it. I'm not like my father, and Lucinda isn't like her mother. We are all different people who have lived with humans, and we act like them.

Why will you stoop so low to tell Lucinda that I'm not human? Why are you trying to ruin things, Anya?" Jake asked.

"Ruin, you say? I'm only trying to protect Lucinda. Though fate has made its proclamation, that won't stop me from protecting her against you." Anya fired back at him with rage.

"I'm not evil. I'm Jake. I'm my father's son, but you should realize that we two are different. My father has unique attributes and features, and so do I. Don't try to rope Lucinda and me into the enmity between the queen and my father. Stay clear, and please do not say another word about me to Lucinda, or else you will feel my full wrath. Even if you're the three in one monster, I'm my father's son. I'm a god, the son of the sun. I will bring total doom and damnation to you. Leave Lucinda and me alone," Jake shouted and started to leave when Anya's voice stopped him.

"Do you waste time flexing your powers on people? I dare you, Jake Sun," Anya shouted back at him.

"I'm not like this. You're trying to turn me into what I'm not.

Just stop feeding Lucinda with information. I will break the news of who I am to her. Leave that to me and stay clear of our relationship. No matter how you and the queen and my father try, I will marry Lucinda. It's entire time for a new beginning," Jake said as he stormed off into the inner house.

"Bastard!" Anya said as she disappeared from the sitting room.

****

Lucinda was sitting all alone in the garden when she felt someone touch her, and on turning, she saw it was Anya.

"You're back," Lucinda remarked.

"Yeah, I needed to run some errands, and I'm done with that," Anya replied.

"A quick question: Why do you hate Jake?" Lucinda asked.

"I don't. I don't hate him. You went over to his place to ask questions, right?" Anya asked.

"Yes, I did. I had to. He is human, Anya, he is. I want to have just one human friend, one human friend, that's all I want, and nobody is helping matters. I wouldn't want to grow old surrounded by only the spirits of my beloved. With that, people living around will term me a witch. I need to have one human friend at least." Lucinda said, almost on the verge of tears.

"I'm sorry, I was just looking out for you. Let's say he is too handsome to be a human. That's why I made that statement. I'm sorry." Anya said, cleaning up the tears on Lucinda's eye with the back of her hand.

"Will you help me?" Lucinda asked.

"Sure, I will. If you're happy, then I'm happy too." Anya said as she hugged Lucinda, who held tightly to her.

Lucinda spent what seemed like forever in Anya's embrace before she stood up and went inside.

Anya stayed there for a few minutes before disappearing into thin air.

****

"You're here. How is Lucinda?" the voice of the queen intoned.

"Lucinda is fine, but I need to talk to you about something important. It's about Lucinda." Anya said.

Anya had gone to the moon to consult the queen of the moon and the stars. She needed to explain things to her.

"It's about Jake and Lucinda. Listen, Jake isn't a bad person. Maybe fate has reasons why it paired Lucinda and Jake to be together, and Jake already asked me to stay clear that I'm making things difficult for him." Anya said.

"And do you think you should stay clear?" The voice said as she turned her chair and faced Anya.

"Yes, I need to stay clear, not because of what he said but because Lucinda finds this peace around him. It feels like they have known each other all the time. The more I keep trying to get in between. I'm only hurting Lucinda. Fate has its reasons why it paired both of them together. Perhaps, this will close the bridge of rift that has been created over the ages," Anya replied.

"Prepare my daughter to meet me," The queen said as she stood up and walked out of the throne room.

Anya bowed before taking her to leave.

CHAPTER EIGHT

It was two days until Lucinda's nineteenth birthday, and it was a day Anya knew they had to make the journey. But Anya knew Lucinda wouldn't be an issue. She knew her grandparents would. How would they react if they found out that Lucinda was going on a trip to another world?

Though they had come to be filled in on some supernatural aspects of Lucinda, leaving earth on a journey to a different world entirely would be difficult for them.

Anya was sitting alone in the garden when she saw Greg walk into the garden and sat close to her.

"The only friend, my grandchild, has, you didn't go on a stroll with Lucinda?" Greg remarked.

"No, I'm here, trying to fix one or two things." Anya replied as Greg looked around and said, "but you're not busy."

"Oh no, not that actually, but can I ask you a question?" Anya asked.

"Surc. Go ahead," Greg commented.

"Will you be okay if Lucinda leaves the house for a five-day trip for something fundamental?" Anya asked.

"I doubt it, but Maya will never agree even if I say yes. We have grown to love Lucinda, and we have become so used to her that we can't spend a day without seeing her. We know someday she will get married and leave the house. She is old enough to decide, but we will be hurt if we don't get to see Lucinda, even if it's just for a day," Greg replied.

"What if she gets married tomorrow? She isn't going to live here forever, you know?" Anya quipped.

"Yea, you're right. When we lost Annalise and Phil, it was a challenging moment for us, but we tried to stay strong and act happy. Lucinda's presence matters a lot to us. We know that someday she will get married and move into her husband's home, but until then," Greg replied, raising his hands in the air.

Lucinda, who was on her way back, met with Jake in the company of two men. As soon as Jake saw her, she excused himself and walked up to her.

"Lucinda, how are you, and where are you going?" Jake asked, trying to hold her hand.

"I'm good; I'm heading back home," Lucinda replied.

"Okay, I wanted to ask. Can I come over tomorrow, Saturday?" Jake asked.

"Sure, why not? You're always welcome, and thanks for the gift.

I haven't been opportune to meet you to tell you to thank you," Lucinda replied.

"That's not an issue. Take good care of yourself," Jake said as he smiled and walked away to rejoin the men with him.

Lucinda smiled as she walked back home. When she got home that evening, she chit-chatted with her parents and grandparents during dinner. She could eat a little food, and when she was questioned, she claimed she was okay.

"Will you and Grandpa ever permit me to sleep out for five days?" Lucinda asked as Maya and Greg looked at each other.

"Where are you going?" Maya asked.

"I'm not going anywhere yet, just asking a question. I want to know like you and Grandpa won't see me for maybe five to six days. Will that be okay with you both?" Lucinda asked again.

"Oh no, we won't be okay with that. You barely know anyone here, or is it with Jake?" Maya asked.

"No, it's not Jake. Why will I stay in Jake's house for five whole days? That's insane. I agree that I like him, but I'm not obsessed with him." Lucinda replied.

"So, to where then?" Greg asked.

"Just a question, so will you both permit me, even if you do not know where?" Lucinda asked, a bit impertinent.

"The answer then is no," Maya said flatly.

"Grandpa, aren't you going to say something? Lucinda asked, looking at Greg.

"I'm with your grandma on this. I know we have lived here for a few years now, but Lucinda, the only person you know, is Jake. So how do you think we would permit you to leave the house? To where?" Greg replied.

"I'm turning nineteen in the next two days. I will still leave you, people, someday." Lucinda replied as she continued nibbling at her food.

Soon she was done with her food as she got up from the chair to tidy up the table, after which she walked straight to the sitting room.

Not long after, Lucinda said goodnight to her parents and grandparents as she walked into her room to sleep. She had a stressful day, and there was no way she could stay awake until midnight. She knew her grandparents were going to stay awake so they could talk and touch Annalise and Phil.

Lucinda lay on the bed as she kept thinking about Jake, being particularly disturbed about her identity, worried about how he would react to finding out she wasn't human. She knew there was no way she would be friends with Jake while still hiding the truth about her identity.

"How do I even get to tell him that I'm not full human? How do I tell him that Anya isn't a human too? How do I reveal to him my true identity? It's so difficult to say this to him. He might not believe me, or he might believe me but will never want to associate with me again," Lucinda groaned.

She was so confused about how to go about everything. For the first time in her life, she was making a human friend; and was now confronted with its associated dilemma, she thought. Or would she rather keep sealed lips about it all?

"How hard can this be!" Lucinda exclaimed and sighed at the same time.

"You looked worried," the voice said as Lucinda turned to see her mom's ghost.

"You're here," Lucinda asked, sitting up.

"I knew something was eating you up, and I had to come. I couldn't ask you in the presence of my parents. That's why I had to wait for you to come to your room so I could talk to you. So, is it okay to tell me what the problem is?" Annalise asked.

"It's Jake, Mom. I'm so confused. He has shown to be a good friend these past months, and he has told me everything I need to know about him, but the problem is I'm not being fair to him." Lucinda replied.

"How do you mean you're not being fair to him?" Annalise asked.

"Mom, can't you see? I'm not fully human. Someday, Jake will find out the truth about who I am, but the question is will he stay on finding out? I feel like telling him the truth, but on the other hand, I don't want to say a word to him. I don't want him to learn about the truth someday and decide to leave. I'm scared. He is the first human friend I have ever made," Lucinda surmised.

"Do you want to tell him who you are?" Annalise asked.

"I don't even know whether to tell him or keep a sealed lip, but I feel that he won't want to stay. He will leave," Lucinda replied.

"Don't dwell on hasty conclusions. You're not Jake. I won't ask you to tell him or keep him shut, but if you think he is a friend, maybe I think you know the right thing to do. A friend should know everything about you. Even if you decide to tell him and he leaves, don't worry. That would be enough to know the friendship wasn't meant to last anyway. But before then, make sure he is qualified to behold in the breath of that word called 'friend' before you spill anything to him," Annalise said.

"Thank you, Mom. I just wish I could hug you right away. Thank you so much. I wonder how life would have been without a mom by my side," Lucinda said.

"You're welcome, my darling. Don't worry. Go to bed. I know you're stressed up. It's written all over you. You can still get to hug me tomorrow or, if you're lucky, wake up early in the morning," Annalise said.

"Goodnight, Mom," Lucinda enthused before lying down and closing her eyes in sleep.

****

"When is she going to tell me the truth? Haven't I proven to be a better friend all these months? I've told her everything she needs to know, except that I'm the sun's son. Doesn't she consider me worthy of telling me everything about her, though I already know? Why is she scared of opening up to me? What could be the reason?" Jake pondered as he stared at the sky.

Jake has been up all night, thinking about Lucinda, feeling that she needed to hear the truth about her, which would prove that she trusted him.

"You're awake, thinking about her. What have you turned into, Jake?" The voice asked.

"Not again, father. I can think of anyone I want to. Besides, I'm not feeling sleepy," Jake responded.

"I see. Go to bed, Jake. She will tell you who she is by herself when she is ready," the voice ordered.

"Thank you, Father, but I will sleep later. You're not helping matters," Jake said.

"I don't like her, neither do I like her mother, so why will I help you get someone I don't like?" the voice asked.

"You and Lucinda's mother need help. This girl has done nothing to you. It isn't her fault she is the daughter of the moon and the stars, and it isn't my fault I'm your son, either. We are both different people, and I think fate made us fall in love with each other to solve the age-long schism between you and Lucinda's mother. Think about this. Good night, Father," Jake said as he stood up, locking the window to his room, and soon after he lay on the bed, he drifted off to sleep.

****

Jake stood at the door as he tried knocking, but he refrained from doing so on second thought. Too many ideas were running through his mind, and just when he turned to leave, the door flung open as Maya walked out.

"Jake, you're here. How are you doing?" Maya asked.

"I'm good, and how about you?" Jake asked.

"I'm fine. I guess you're here to see Lucinda. Go to the stable. She is feeding the horses. You can go and see her there." Maya said.

"Thanks," Jake smiled as he walked down to the backyard. On getting there, Jake saw that the stable was locked, which meant that Lucinda was through with feeding the horses. He knew the next place Lucinda would be in the garden. He then strolled down; and met Lucinda watering the gardens.

"The flowers look so fresh and beautiful," Jake said as Lucinda turned and smiled on seeing him.

"Seems your favorite is the Lily flower," Jake asked as Lucinda nodded as she continued watering the flowers.

She took the can and placed it at the far end before sitting close to Jake on the stone chair when she finished.

"So, tell me, how are you doing?" Lucinda asked.

"I'm good. No need to ask you as I see you are doing just fine," Jake asked as Lucinda smiled.

"Has it been a long time since you got here?" Lucinda asked.

"No, I met your grandma at the door, and she told me you were feeding the horses. When I checked the stable and saw it was locked. I knew you were going to be here," Jake replied.

"Yeah, I just decided to water the flowers. Their colors add beauty to this garden," Lucinda replied.

"Yea. That's nice of you," Jake responded.

"I'm traveling. I won't be around for five or six days. I'm leaving with Anya," Lucinda stated.

"Oh, but what about your grandparents?" Jake asked.

"They are here. I'm still going to come back, not leaving forever." Lucinda replied as Jake nodded.

"Is everything okay? You don't look happy," Lucinda asked.

"I'm fine, just having this sad feeling that I won't get to see you for a couple of days," Jake replied.

"Are you sure that's all? It seems you're bothered about something else. You can tell me what it is," Lucinda asked.

"Lucinda, aside from the trip you're going, isn't there something else you need to tell me?" Jake asked.

"Anything like?" Lucinda queried.

"I don't know, but I feel you want to say something to me," Jake replied.

"No, nothing," Lucinda replied as she kept thinking about what Jake said, wondering whether he had by himself found out her true identity. Soon she became alarmed at what could be the outcome of such a revelation.

On seeing that Lucinda was lost in thought, Jake decided to bring her to the present by giving her a nudge. He had tried to get her attention by calling her name thrice, but she did not respond. Lucinda sat up straight after.

"What were you thinking? About what I said? I called you thrice, and when you didn't respond, I had to touch you, is everything okay," Jake asked.

"Yeah, I'm okay," Lucinda assured.

"No, you're not okay. It's written over you. What's the problem?" Jake asked to hope that Lucinda would use the opportunity to spill the truth, but instead, she still kept shut about it.

"Don't worry, I'm fine. Just thinking about some random things and also about my grandparents. But about what you said earlier, I already told you everything you need to know. I'm not hiding anything more. So, you don't need to worry." Lucinda said, smiling as Jake nodded.

"Alright, that's okay," Jake replied.

The duo was discussing when Anya walked in and greeted Jake, but Jake kept mute and made as if he didn't hear her greeting.

"I will be leaving now," Jake announced as he stood up and walked out immediately. It wasn't any use staying there for him since Anya was already there with her. He didn't even wait for Lucinda to say a word.

"Why is he leaving?" Anya asked, feigning surprise.

"Because of you, I guess. I wonder why you hate and despise him so much." Lucinda asked.

"He is the one who hates me," Anya said.

"No, it's not true. I know Jake, and I know you. He sees you as a threat because you don't want him to get close to me, which is true, but why, Anya? Jake is all shade of handsome and nice." Lucinda said.

"Perhaps both of us don't like each other. Your grandmother wants you inside for lunch," Anya tersely said.

"But you haven't answered my question; why do you hate him?" Lucinda asked.

"I don't hate him; I hate his guts," Anya said as she stood up and walked into the house. Lucinda sighed and followed suit, trying to understand what Anya meant.

"Oh, I thought you were with Jake. Where is he?" Maya asked.

"Oh, Jake. He left." Anya replied.

"Why didn't he even come in to greet me?" Greg asked.

"Something came up suddenly, so he had to leave quickly." Lucinda lied.

"Let's eat then," Maya said as they all sat down while Maya dished out the food.

****

"I'm sure Anya is preventing Lucinda from spilling the truth. She swore to make life miserable for me, and she is at it. I just hate her." Jake cursed as he strolled down home.

When Jake got home, he walked straight to his bedroom and sat down on the bed.

"Why don't you give up on this girl?" the voice asked.

"I can't, father, I can't. Aside from the prophecy, I have grown to love Lucinda. I don't know why she finds it hard to open herself completely to me." Jake responded.

"Perhaps she doesn't love you enough." The voice said.

"Or maybe she doesn't trust me enough. Telling someone she feels is a human being and that she is the daughter of the moon and the stars are huge. That's the exact reason. As for loving me? I know Lucinda loves me," Jake replied.

"Well, when are you coming home?" The voice asked.

"When Lucinda is ready to go home," Jake replied.

"You have allowed this girl to take a better part of you. You mean to hate her and not love her." The voice added.

"Father, can you please stop. I know you and the queen are arch enemies. And she already had accepted the prophecy. Why can't you do the same? There is nothing to hate in Lucinda. That girl is innocent, naive, and without stain. I'm glad fate brought us together," Jake responded.

"I need to go and rest, but I just want you to come home soon," the voice replied.

"I can't come home without leaving a child on this planet. You know that already," Jake responded.

"The time is ticking. You barely have up to four decades remaining. I need you home. You have a world to rule here," the voice said as Jake groaned and fell back on the bed, mentally exhausted.

****

"It's just for a few days. Not like I'm spending a whole year there," Lucinda said.

Lucinda found it hard to convince her grandparents about the trip she needed to make. She had to visit the world she was from.

"You might go there and decide not to come home. How do you think we would let you leave? It's your birthday today. For the past eight years, we have always celebrated your birthday together. So why will today be different?" Maya asked.

"No, why will you even think of that? This is still my home. Mom and Dad are here. You and Grandpa are here. So, why will I stay in another world? And of course, I know it's my birthday, the more reason I need to leave today. Please understand me." Lucinda begged.

"Truth is that we're scared. Things might go wrong. If you leave and don't come back, I won't survive it." Greg added.

"I swear by the moon and the stars. I will come home." Lucinda pledged.

"She has already mentioned the moon and the stars. So, I know she will come back. Just let her go." Phil said.

"Phil is right. Let Lucinda go. She will come back, and she means it," Annalise added.

"I promise to bring her back. We need to leave today. I swear by the moon and the stars," Anya said as Maya rushed and hugged Lucinda tightly as tears trickled down her cheeks.

Greg went closer to them as he hugged them too. Lucinda's absence would hit them hard, even if it were a temporal absence.

"I promise, I will be home in six days," Lucinda assured again. The words were scarcely out of her mouth when Anya touched her, and they both disappeared right before everyone present. Maya and Greg hugged each other as Maya cried in her husband's arms. Annalise and Phil had to console them.

****

Anya and Lucinda approached the entrance to the world of the moon and the stars. Lucinda couldn't help but stare at the magnificent gate right in front of her, which was made of pure gold, glistening from the incandescence of the moon.

"Are you ready to meet your home?" Anya asked as Lucinda nodded.

Anya pushed the gate slowly as they both walked in. Lucinda's jaw dropped as she stared at the new world unfolding before her.

"You mean I'm from here?" Lucinda asked with her eyes and mouth wide open.

"Yes, welcome home, Lucinda," Anya enthused.

"This place is beyond description. Saying it's beautiful is a mockery. It's beyond beautiful; it's amazing," Lucinda said as she stared at the beautiful flowers and creatures moving about.

"Let's go," Anya said as she held Lucinda's hand, and they both walked into the city made of gold.

Lucinda watched as the men standing at the entrance bowed to them. One of them quickly opened the door.

Lucinda was dumbfounded and weak to utter a word. She turned sideways, admiring the environment before as she stood beside a castle, grand and regale beyond her infantile mind could ever imagine.

"Let me guess, this is home, right?" Lucinda asked, pointing to the castle as Anya nodded.

Soon, Lucinda felt a hand touch her as she quietly turned to see who it was. Lucinda was shocked to see a woman standing before her. She was the fairest of them, and she noticed this striking resemblance with the woman. Her skin was as white as snow. Her hair as white as wool. She was aging beautifully.

"Welcome home, my child," The woman said as Lucinda raised her hands and touched the woman's face, who smiled in return.

"Are you the woman whose loins I came out from?" Lucinda

asked as the woman nodded.

"What's your name?" Lucinda asked.

"Salle, Queen Salle," she replied.

"Would it be okay if I call you mother or Queen Salle," Lucinda asked as Queen Salle smiled and answered, "anyone can do?"

"Thank you, Anya, for a job well done. You took great care of her, and I'm impressed," Queen Salle commended as Anya smiled, saying in between smiles, "thank you, my Queen."

"You may leave," Queen Salle said as Anya swiftly changed into a werewolf and raced out of the palace.

"Is she coming back?" Lucinda asked.

"Of course, but not now. I have a lot to show you, daughter," Queen Salle said as Lucinda nodded.

Queen Salle walked down the pathway quietly as Lucinda followed suit. When they got to a door, Queen Salle pushed it open slowly.

Lucinda was shocked to see something like the moon hanging right there in the room while its light illuminated the entire room.

"What is this? It's beautiful, and it's huge," Lucinda asked.

"Touch it and tell me what you see," Queen Salle responded.

Lucinda looked at the queen for something that seemed an eternity before stretching her hand to touch the moon. And no sooner had her hand felt it than she started seeing a series of visions.

"What will you call what you saw? Good or evil?" Queen Salle asked as soon as Lucinda recovered from her shock.

"I don't know. Instead of you, I was the one sitting on your throne. My parents didn't stay with me for long in the human world, and I saw my grandparents leaving," Lucinda asked.

"I'm aging, Lucinda. Someone has to take the throne when I'm no more. The moon chose you, your parents, and your grandparents. They are not leaving now, but someday they will because they need to come back and prepare for the coming of their new queen. This place is your home. You're not going to stay on the earth forever. And then when you age too, one of your children will be chosen to take over from you," Queen Salle replied.

Lucinda didn't utter a word as she walked closer to the moon, stared at it, and asked silently.

"Why aren't you showing me anything about Jake? Perhaps now is the time to tell me."

"When you get back to earth, you and Jake have to conclude whether you will end up together," Queen Salle said as Lucinda turned and asked, "how did you hear that?"

"You're asking me that? What did I not know? You don't know everything, child. Don't worry. Once you ascend that throne, the powers will be transferred to you, but for now, I can see that this

Jake is making you happy. He is the luckiest man to have you," Queen Salle responded, as Lucinda blushed.

"I can't tell him anything about me. I want to, and on the other hand, I don't want to. I'm confused. He deserves to know the truth. He has felt that I'm hiding something from him. We met before I came here, and when he insinuated that, I was sad. I knew I was guilty, but how do I explain that I'm not who he thinks I am? He will leave me if he finds out who I am," Lucinda said with a teary voice.

"Tell him and allow him to decide for himself," Queen Salle replied.

Lucinda moved closer to Queen Salle as she hugged her tightly, saying, "I have two mothers, one here and the other on earth. I have done many things for her, and I hope someday I will do something in return for all my wishes you granted."

Queen Salle smiled as she said, "You're my daughter, and I have to make life easier for you on earth."

"Thank you, Mom," Lucinda said, smiling.

"Anya will be here any moment from now to take you home," Queen Salle said.

"But it's not even up to four hours that we got here?" Lucinda asked.

"The time here differs from earth. You have been away for your days on earth. Your grandparents are already missing you. They want you home as soon as possible," Queen Salle replied.

"I didn't know that's how it works here," Lucinda said.

Queen Salle removed her necklace as she put it on Lucinda, same with her bracelet, which had the moon and the stars' symbol.

"Subsequently, don't remove. Always wear them. Promise me you do that," Queen Salle said.

"I promise. I won't take them off," Lucinda said, smiling.

"Let's go then," Queen Salle said as she held Lucinda's hand, and they both walked out of the room together. Anya was already waiting in the throne room.

"Anya!" Lucinda called as he walked closer to Lucinda and hugged her.

"Thank you for keeping her safe on earth." Queen Salle said.

"You're welcome, my queen. It's my duty. I can't watch any harm befall on the queen's beloved." Anya replied.

"Thank you. You will take Lucinda back home. It's already time to leave. An hour over here is a day over there. Her grandparents are already missing her. They want her home badly." Queen Salle said as Anya bowed, after which the queen came closer to Anya and Lucinda, holding their hands tightly, as she murmured some strange words, which prompted them into fading into thin air. She had sent them back to earth.

Lucinda was surprised to see herself in her bedroom.

"Home is beautiful. I can't believe that's where I came from." Lucinda said as Anya smiled and said, "I know you will make a better queen someday."

Lucinda smiled as she walked out of the bedroom together with Anya. Maya was shocked to see Lucinda standing next to her. Lucinda had to hug her while still sitting as she tried standing up.

"I'm glad you're home. I thought you wouldn't come back ever again." Maya said with a teary voice.

"I'm home. This is my home," Lucinda replied.

"Where is Grandpa, Greg?" Anya asked.

"Oh, he is sleeping and..."

"I'm awake now," Greg said, coming out of the door as Lucinda rushed to where he was standing and hugged him tightly.

"Thank you for coming home," Greg said.

"This is my home. I can't leave. A part of me still lives here." Lucinda replied.

"Jake was here in the morning. He asked about you and I told him you will be back soon." Maya said.

"Jake? Okay. I will see him this evening," Lucinda said, smiling.

"Let me quickly prepare something nice," Maya said as she stood up and walked into the kitchen.

"I know my mom and dad aren't here now, and they should be back soon. Tell them I will be home soon. Let me see Jake," Lucinda said as she raced out of the house. She didn't even wait to hear Anya or her grandfather's reply before leaving.

When Lucinda got to Jake's apartment, she stood at the door and knocked; and after some minutes, the door flung open as Jake walked out.

He was shocked to see Lucinda standing right in front of him; as he quickly hugged her.

"I know it's belated, but I can still wish you a happy birthday. I have missed you so much." Jake whispered into Lucinda's ear.

"Same here," Lucinda said, smiling as they walked into the sitting room, holding each other tightly.

◆ ◆ ◆

CHAPTER NINE

Anya walked into Lucinda's room to meet her, lost in her thoughts. She just stood watching her and admiring her at the same time. But soon after, she tried calling her attention, but it seemed her mind wasn't in that room anymore.

Anya sat on the edge of the bed, and stretching her hand, she touched Lucinda, who instantly came back to the present. She did that a second time, yet Lucinda received no response.

"How long have you been here?" Lucinda asked.

"For over three minutes now, I called you twice, but you were thinking about something else. Is there any problem?" Anya asked.

"Yeah, aren't you noticing her absence? She meant to visit regularly, but it's been months now since she visited last. Do you think I wronged her? I can easily ask for forgiveness if I did so," Lucinda said while wearing a mournful look.

"You mean Amber?" Anya asked.

"Yes, I'm dying to see her. It's been such a long time, and it hurts not seeing her. We spent time here every night; she is part of us. She is family, but suddenly, she isn't here anymore. Isn't that strange?" Lucinda asked.

"Yeah, now I understand where you are heading," Anya said.

"You know, I miss Amber. It's been months since I last saw her. Why isn't she coming around anymore? I thought she promised she would often visit? Why isn't she keeping to her promise?" Lucinda asked.

"Lucia, I know..."

Wait, what did you just call me?" Lucinda asked, surprised.

"I called you Lucia," Anya replied as Lucinda smiled.

"Listen, I know you want to see Amber, by all means. I also know you're dying to meet her, but you should know that Amber isn't like you and me. She has limited time to be on this earth."

"I can still "

"You can't do anything about it, Lucinda. Some wishes can't be granted. You don't have to worry. Eventually, Amber will come around, then she will explain so you will understand. You were with her for a long time, so I'm sure you both understand yourself better." Anya replied.

"If she is going to come, she has to come soon. It's been months without her," Lucinda replied.

"Don't worry; you will be fine," Anya said as she stood up to leave, but Lucinda called her back.

"Are you leaving me all alone?" Lucinda asked.

"Maybe you should visit Jake if you need company, and I think you do. I'm not going inside. I'm going to the bushes," Anya replied as Lucinda smiled on hearing Anya's suggestion. She watched as Anya faded into thin air. But Lucinda did not go anywhere. She stayed in her room all day, tossing around her bed. In the evening, Anya walked into her room to meet her still lying on the bed. She stood in the doorway, staring at her.

"Why are you looking at me that way?" Lucinda asked.

"Amber is leaving. She is here to say her final goodbye." Anya dropped the news as Lucinda stood up immediately and rushed into the sitting room to see Amber with her grandparents.

"Amber, you know you can't stop visiting. You're like a family to us. I want to keep seeing you. You can't just come to say goodbye. It's not fair," Lucinda whined.

"I wanted the same too, but you know that's impossible. We are two different beings. I have to go and rest, but I'm going to make a promise to you when you birth your first child. I will come to you as a daughter. Remember that." Amber said.

"But that's going to be a long time. Can't you see how miserable I am? Please stay because of me," Lucinda said with a teary voice.

"She has to go, Lucinda. I know this will be hard for you to take in, but you just have to accept it. Don't worry. With time you will get used to her absence. She promised she would be coming back as a child in from your loins," Annalise said.

"It's hard letting her go. I can't imagine I won't see her face anymore," Lucinda said as tears trickled down her cheeks.

"It's going to be fine. You just have to hold on to the good memories you both shared," Annalise said.

"Your mother is right. Crying will never solve the problem. Just believe that someday she will come back," Phil consoled.

"It's easier said than done. How do I cope without her?" Lucinda asked.

"Your grandmother and I are here with you, your parents, can't you see?" Greg asked, hoping to bring in a measure of consolation for Lucinda.

"Please, Lucinda, clean your tears. They are hurting me. I hate seeing you like this. You just have to think of the good times you shared, please," Maya pleaded.

"Lucinda, please listen to them. I will be back soon," Amber said as Lucinda rushed and hugged her tightly.

"When you're ready to bring forth seed into this world, I will come as your first child," Amber assured.

"I know you mean it, but it's hard letting go," Lucinda said.

"Don't worry. I will be here sooner than you imagine," Amber said as she slowly wiped the tears off Lucinda's eyes.

As Amber walked closer to the door, she turned and waved goodbye to Lucinda and her family before disappearing into thin air. Lucinda fell into her grandmother's arms as she cried bitterly while they all tried consoling her.

****

"Your heart is heavy. You're questioning yourself on the right thing to do. To crown it all, you're confused. Hey, look at me." Jake said as he gently placed his hands on Lucinda's face and said, "you know you can confide in me. What's the problem?"

Life with Jake these past few months had been one of the best moments ever for Lucinda. Lucinda was still worried about how Jake would react if he learned the truth about who she was. She wanted to spill the truth, but on the other hand, she tried to protect her friendship at all costs.

"You're not saying anything? I'm still waiting for your response," Jake said, looking deep into her eyes.

"I want to talk to you about something important, but the truth is, I don't know how you're " Lucinda paused as she groaned in frustration while Jake waited patiently for her to finish up her sentence. But when it was clear, she wasn't going to say anything else. Jake had to break the silence.

"What do you want to tell me, and why aren't you saying anything? Can't you see how miserable you are looking? You want to spill it out, yet you are afraid to talk," Jake said.

"You don't understand and... "

"I understand everything, Lucinda. But then, if you knew what friendship is all about, if I meant a lot to you, you wouldn't be hiding anything from me. Look around, I'm the only friend you have, and also, you're the only friend I have. What makes you think your secret isn't safe with me?" Jake asked.

Turning sharply, Lucinda asked, "How do you know it's a secret?"

"Don't try to divert from the main topic. Of course, it's a secret because you're finding it hard to say it. Perhaps, when you consider me a friend, I will know, but I think I'm just a neighbor leaving down the road for now. Take good care of yourself, Lucinda," Jake said as he stood up and left.

Lucinda tried calling him back, but he ignored her and hurried away. Lucinda sat back on the chair as tears found their way to her cheeks.

"What have I done? I have pushed out the only friend I have. Will I ever forgive myself?" Lucinda asked with a teary voice.

When Lucinda couldn't take it anymore, she ran into the house and went straight to her room. She locked the door and placed a spell on it. That way, not even Anya or her parent's spirit will have access to the room. She didn't want to see or talk to anyone. She just wanted to be alone.

"What have I just done? What have I done to myself? How do I tell him the truth? Now I only have two options: tell him and save my friendship or keep shut and lose him forever.

What if I told him and he left? And what if he didn't leave? These past few months, I have grown to love him. The only human who has proved to be a good friend," Lucinda groaned.

Lucinda couldn't imagine losing her only friend. She knew she had to explain herself to Jake somehow, because keeping shut would ruin everything. Lucinda was still in her riot of thoughts when she noticed Anya was trying to gain access to the bedroom. She had to lift the spell, and just immediately, Anya appeared in the room.

"What's the problem? Why did you prevent me from gaining access to your room? What's wrong?" Anya asked, but as soon as he saw Lucinda in tears, she walked up to her and dried the tears.

"What's wrong? You were with Jake a few minutes ago, and now you're here crying your eyes out. What's the problem?" Anya asked.

"It's Jake," Lucinda said amidst sobs.

"I knew that boy was up to no good. How dare he...?"

"Anya, he didn't do anything," Lucinda said, cutting Anya short.

"If he didn't do anything, why are you in tears? Why are you covering up for him?" Anya asked.

"I'm not covering up for him. Whatever happens between Jake and me is my entire fault. Can't you see he has been kind and good and nice towards me all this while? He has proven to be a good human.

He accepted me with his hands wide open, and what did I do? I kept a vital part of my secret from him. I think he has noticed that I'm hiding something from him, and today when he couldn't take it anymore, he left. Even when I tried calling him back, he didn't stop.

He acted as if he didn't even hear the sound of my voice. I guess I have lost the only friend," Lucinda said with a teary voice.

"No, you didn't lose him. I'm sure he will come around. He is angry, but you can forget about him and move on if he doesn't. He isn't the only one here on earth, or is there any other thing you aren't telling me?" Anya asked.

Lucinda didn't say anything. Instead, she lay down on her bed, covering herself up. On seeing that, Anya smiled as she walked out of the room.

****

Jake got home and went straight to dish out something to eat. He was so mad at Lucinda. He was furious and sad that Lucinda didn't trust him enough to tell him everything.

"Hey!" the voice said as Jake looked back and sighed.

"Just because you have powers doesn't give you the audacity to come into my house anytime, any day. Have some respect," Jake scowled.

"I had to come; it's necessary. I just wanted to ask a few questions. Then I'm out of here," Anya replied.

"What do you want?" Jake asked.

"I want to ask why you're selfish, proud, and arrogant? The fact that you are the son of the sun doesn't place you above everyone," Anya said.

"Proud and arrogant? I know I'm not that, but what do you mean by selfish? What did I do? I know I have done absolutely nothing to get that appellation from you." Jake replied.

"Oh really? Then why can't you come clean and tell Lucinda the truth? Tell Lucinda who you are. You don't have to wait for her to tell you who she is, or is it recorded anywhere that Lucinda must be the first to spill the truth about her real identity?

And as if that wasn't enough, you made her lock herself up and cry like she lost someone dear to her. What manner of human are you? Ever since I have known Lucinda, I have never seen her this way. All I can say is I hate you for this. I don't know what you said to her, but I want you to go back and apologize," Anya said.

"Force me if you can, but I'm certain I didn't use any mean words on Lucinda. She is crying because she lost a friend in me.

When I said so, I meant it. I showed Lucinda my world. I told her everything she needed to know aside from the fact that I'm the son of the sun which I'm waiting for the day she turns twenty before I can tell her, but since you are too eager for her to know the truth about me, I will meet up with her and tell her, and after that, I'm gone. Now you can leave my house, Anya, and don't you ever come back," Jake said.

"How sure am I that you're not going to return someday?" Anya asked, a little excited about hearing Jake's words.

"You and your queen have always wanted that, and my father. So, exiting Lucinda's life will make you all the happiest. I want to go into my room, and when I'm out, I don't want to see you here," Jake said as he stood up and walked into his room.

"I hate his guts. I wish he leaves and never comes back," Anya howled.

****

"I thought you left? Or you came back for me?" Lucinda asked as she saw Amber sitting calmly on the edge of the bed.

"You need help. Why are you still delaying telling him the truth about who you are? Stop thinking of what will happen if you eventually tell him. Tell him and save yourself all this stress," Amber said.

"It's not that easy, Amber. I might lose him. He might leave me, or worst he might tell people who I am. I wouldn't want what happened years ago to repeat itself." Lucinda replied.

"You don't want to tell him, yet you don't want to lose your friendship. It's so obvious that you're hiding something from him, and he already noticed that. Now, tell me, what do you think of Jake?" Amber asked.

"Jake is all shade of nice, good, and humble. He possesses all the good characteristics one needs in a human being. He is a good friend, and I value our friendship," Lucinda said.

"What if you keep shut and end up losing your friendship? I doubt you value your friendship because you will tell him everything if you do. Just talk to him, so you don't lose everything," Amber said.

"I will try. I'm glad you're here." Lucinda said as she stretched her hands to hug Amber, who faded into thin air.

Lucinda looked around and called Amber's name, but there was no response. She slowly opened her eyes to see that she was dreaming. "Amber came to visit in my dreams. Yes, she was here. Ooh, Amber!" Lucinda said as she smiled.

"Lucinda, are you okay?" Maya asked as she walked into Lucinda's room.

"Yeah, I'm okay," Lucinda replied.

"But you were smiling a few seconds ago, and I'm sure you just woke up. So, why are you smiling?" Maya asked.

"Amber paid a visit to me in my dream. It was nice seeing her face again," Lucinda replied.

"That's nice; you should smile often. When you're done with whatever you're doing here, come to the sitting room, okay?" Maya said as Lucinda nodded.

****

She enjoyed the gentle breeze and the silence when she heard the voice. Lucinda slowly opened her eyes to see Jake standing right in front of her.

"You are here," Lucinda remarked with her eyes wide open.

"I came to tell you what you need to know. You deserve to know before I leave," Jake said.

"You can at least sit. What do you want to say, and what do you mean before you leave?" Lucinda asked.

"Don't worry; I should stand up. I'm not going to waste much time here." Jake replied.

"What's the problem, Jake? Is everything alright?" Lucinda asked.

"Yeah, I just want to tell you the truth. You know Anya was right when she said I'm not a human and..."

"Wait. Wait. What are you talking about, and how did you know Anya said that?" Lucinda asked with her brows raised high.

"The truth is, I'm not a human. I'm a God. I don't even consider myself half-human because I wasn't born to be a human. Let me break it down. This couple has been childless for years, and throughout their lives, they have been worshipping the sun.

Before my mother passed, she handed me over to these human parents because she was sure my father wouldn't take care of me the way she wanted. I grew up with them thinking I was human, and just when I was ten, I realized who I was and why I was there with them. Life was perfect here. I didn't want to go back to where I came from. I stayed back.

But I always pay a visit to my father. After a few years, my earthy parents died in their sleep. I didn't want to go back home. I stayed here, and I was already used to being with humans.

Whenever I visit home, I feel like a stranger because I barely know who my people are. So, this is me. This is the real Jake. Therefore, my eyes are like pure gold. Anya called me selfish, proud, and arrogant, but I'm not any of those, and I sure know that your parent's ghost lives with you. If you consider me a friend, you should have opened up and told me who you are, but I won't force you since you're adamant and won't tell anyone. Take good care of yourself, Lucinda. Extend my greetings to your grandparents," Jake said as he turned to leave, but Lucinda called him back.

"You're saying you're the son of the sun!" Lucinda asked, with eyes wide open.

"That I already explained; take good care of yourself, Lucinda. I'm leaving," Jake said.

"Where are you going?" Lucinda asked.

"I don't know, and thank you for the little memories we created together." And with that, Jake stormed out of the place ablaze.

Lucinda was speechless. She just didn't know how to take in the news that Jake had just told her.

"So, Anya knew all this while. That's why she has been harsh to Jake."

Lucinda realized herself when she noticed that someone had touched her. Looking back, she saw it was Anya.

"You have been overthinking these days. I called you twice, but no response from you." Anya said.

"You knew he was the son of the sun, and you didn't tell me?" Lucinda asked.

"I tried giving you a hint, but you didn't get that. I guess he told you already. I was waiting for him to tell you," Anya replied.

"But you should have explained better," Lucinda said.

"It wasn't in my place to tell you. Now that he told you who he is, did you tell him who you are?" Anya asked.

"No, I didn't. Since he is the son of the sun, he should know who I am. He kept shut about his identity for months," Lucinda answered.

"Don't be too sure that he knows who you are. He already came clean. I think you should do the same," Anya said as she stood up and left the garden.

Lucinda sighed as she rested her back on the chair while different thoughts ran through his mind. She just couldn't believe what she heard right now. She could take it in that all this while she had been friends with a god.

****

Lucinda stood at the door as she tried knocking, but there was no response. She then looked at Anya, who looked away.

"We have been standing here for over ten minutes, and he won't open the door," Lucinda said.

"That's because he isn't at home."

"How did you know? We have been standing here together." Lucinda remarked.

"You're Lucinda, and I'm Anya. When you master your powers, then your soul can be able to leave your body for a few minutes just like I did and went into Jake's apartment to see he isn't in, and he hasn't been there for over a week now," Anya replied as Lucinda's face turned white immediately.

"You're joking, right?" Lucinda said as she shivered.

"What part exactly do you think I'm joking about?" Anya asked.

"About him not to have been in this place for over a week now," Lucinda answered.

"Jake isn't even in this town. Let's go home, Lucinda. Maybe he has gone back to where he came from," Anya added.

"That's not fair. He can't leave like that. This isn't fair. Was that why he said he needed to tell me the truth before leaving? So, he meant it when he said he was leaving? I tried to find out what he meant, but he was adamant about leaving. He wouldn't even say a word to me. He doesn't have to leave like that," Lucinda said, almost on the verge of tears.

"Lucinda, please don't; not now," Anya pleaded.

"Will he ever come back?" Lucinda asked.

"I don't have the answer to that, Lucinda. Jake might or may never come back to this town. Why hope for the best? You can still expect the worst. I'm sorry," Anya said.

"You're right. Let's go home," Lucinda said.

Anya held her as they both walked down the road. No sooner had they gotten to the house than Lucinda locked herself up in her room while soaking herself in her tears, wondering how she could live with the guilt of not opening up to Jake before leaving the town.

"Now, I might never get the chance to see him and tell him

everything. I lost a friend, a good one at that. He wasn't like Star. He was a perfect definition of a friend, and now he is gone," Lucinda lamented as tears trickled down her cheeks.

She felt she had made the worst mistake ever and may never forgive herself for losing Jake. Jake only wanted the truth from her, but it was tough for Lucinda to tell.

It had been a month since Jake left. Lucinda had continuously sneaked out of the house for these months to see if Jake had returned home, but the place was still empty.

Lucinda tried to act strong, Though it was clear that Jake's disappearance was taking its toll on her. Soon her grandparents became suspicious when they continuously asked about Jake, but Lucinda would lie to them that Jake had traveled and would be back shortly.

No one knew what was happening because Lucinda always tried to act happy, but she was bleeding and hurting deep down. Anya knew what was wrong, but she couldn't do anything.

At some point, she wished Jake hadn't left. Anya thought Lucinda would be fine, but Jake's absence turned Lucinda into something else. Anya tried to talk to Lucinda, but it fell on deaf ears. She tried searching for Jake, but it was a fruitless search.

On a starry night, Lucinda was staring right at the sky, standing by her window, when she sensed someone moving into her room.

"Is everything okay with you, child?" the voice asked.

"Yes, I'm fine," Lucinda replied.

"You know you can always talk to me. I will understand. I have noticed something very off about you for the last one month. Something is eating you up, but you're trying so hard to hide it from us. I'm your father. Talk to me. I want to share this pain with you." Phil said.

"Don't worry, Father, I'm okay. Eventually, I'm going to sort this out independently. I just need a few more times, and I will get back to my usual self. Trust me," Lucinda said.

"I thought you would get over it soon, but it's over a month now. You don't have to carry this burden all alone. I want to help my child. Tell me what is wrong," Phil asked.

"I'm okay. Don't worry about me. I will be fine," Lucinda replied with his eyes fixed on the sky.

Phil knew better. He knew Lucinda wasn't going to talk. He gently left the room.

Lucinda looked up in the sky and said, "I know you can hear me. Please bring Jake home. I promise I'm going to tell him everything.

Tell him I'm sorry for everything and I still value and miss our friendship if you see him. Life hasn't made any sense ever since he left. I want him back. I know you can do this for me. When you find him, tell him Lucinda said she is sorry."

Tears trickled down her cheeks, but Lucinda didn't bother to clean up as she continued staring at the sky in silence. She knew that something valuable was missing in her life, and she needed to get it back.

****

Jake frowned when the wind brought the message Lucinda had said that night.

"Why does she want me back? She doesn't even see me as a friend. She wants to open up because she hasn't set her eyes on me for a month now. I don't want to come back. I should say here," Jake said.

Jake had gone back to his kingdom because he needed some time off to think about himself and Lucinda.

"I'm proud of you, son. Lucinda isn't worth it," The voice said as Jake turned back and sighed.

"Can you be at least kind to her, father? Maybe she has her reason for keeping it a secret from me. She thought I was a mere human." Jake defended.

"Whatever the reason is, I don't care. If Lucinda loved and valued your friendship, she would have told you long ago, but what did she do? She kept it to herself, which is a sign of distrust." The king replied.

"Father," Jake shouted.

"Yes, that's the truth. I hope you're not going back there? You have been away for too long," The king said as Jake stood up and said, "someday, you will get to like her."

Jake walked out of the room and went straight to the Pinnacle of the building as he stared at the kingdom, which was built with gold, wondering whether to either stay or get back to earth.

◆ ◆ ◆

CHAPTER TEN

"You love him? Don't you? It's written all over your face,"

Greg commented.
Lucinda kept quiet as she observed her grandparents, not desiring to say anything, whether or not in the affirmative. They knew why they asked her whether she was in love with Jake.

Lucinda felt bored staying at home all alone. She wasn't going to sit all day waiting for Jake. She would tell her grandparents she would visit Jake, but she would stop by somewhere else and spend two hours before going home without eventually seeing Jake.

Greg and Maya were happy with the new development, but they didn't want Lucinda to go. They had become so attached to her they couldn't do without seeing her every moment of the day. They never knew what was happening. They thought their grandchild had a perfect relationship with Jake, without knowing that Jake had been away for a while.

"You are already twenty, so you should be free to answer the question. We already asked Jake, and he confessed he loves you so much," Maya started on a cool breezy evening.

"But that's not the problem. The problem is that I don't know how to tell Jake about me and the circumstances of me. How do I explain to him that my parents' ghosts live with us? How do I explain that I'm not who he thinks I am, though he has already told me about himself? He deserves to know the truth. Yes, he does." Lucinda said.

"Don't conclude yet. You haven't even told Jake, and if he can't accept you for who you are, the door is wide open for him to leave. But I know Jake. I know he will understand you. He is different, and I can feel it. You can't keep hiding the truth from him. Come up with ways to talk to him about it," Greg replied.

"But why isn't Jake coming to visit us anymore? Is everything okay?" Greg asked.

"Same here. I meant to ask Lucinda that. Why are you the one visiting him? Why isn't he visiting us like before?" Maya asked.

"What if we decide to visit him instead?" Greg suggested.

"No. There won't be any need for that. Don't worry. Jake will come around. He just wanted to sort out a few things, and he apologized. He said he would visit very soon," Lucinda replied, avoiding eye contact with her grandparents as she quickly changed the topic to something else. She didn't want her grandparents to know the truth, at least not now.

The past two months have been horrible for Lucinda. No matter how hard she tried, she just couldn't get the thought of Jake out of her head. She tried so hard to act strong, but it was apparent that something else was bothering her.

Lucinda excused herself as she went to the garden behind the house. She just sat there as different thoughts ran through her mind.

"I guess you are thinking about him; you miss him," Anya commented as she sat close to Lucinda.

"If there is another word to replace it, I would gladly use it. I miss Jake greatly, and I wish he would come home soon," Lucinda replied.

"Will you tell him about yourself, who you are, and your real identity?" Anya asked.

"Yes, I will. Jake already told me about himself, so why should I hide my identity again? I just wish he would come home. He has to come home," Lucinda affirmed.

"But what if he never comes home?" Anya asked.

"He is not that wicked and heartless to stay there because of the little issue. We didn't even have much of an issue. It was just a minor misunderstanding. Anya, if you knew where he is, tell me. I want to look for him. He has to come home. This is where he belongs," Lucinda pleaded.

"He isn't from this world. He is from the other side," Anya reminded her.

"I know, but this was his first home, so he can't just leave like that. This is still his first home irrespective of whether he isn't from here," Lucinda replied.

"Trust me, I don't know where he is right now, but while hoping for the best. Let's also hope for the worst. He might come back here, and maybe he might never come back. Whichever one happens, you should accept it. And when are you going to tell your grandparents the truth? You can't just keep lying to them. You can't keep leaving the house under the pretense of going out to visit Jake when he has been away for a month. How long do you think you can continue with this?" Anya asked.

"I don't know. That's the truth, Anya. I don't know how long I can continue with this, but I still can't tell them that Jake has been away for months now. I just wish he would be merciful enough to give me a chance to explain myself," Lucinda said.

"Okay, until then. Let's be hopeful," Anya replied as she stood up and left the garden.

Lucinda quickly cleaned the tears off her eyes as she wouldn't want anyone to see her

crying.

"The first time I felt this way was when my parents died. Now, I'm feeling the same way again. I hope you will be kind enough to come home soon," Lucinda said to herself as she stood up and walked inside.

She got to her room as she took out the seashell, and ran her hands on it.

"I don't know if this will work again because I'm asking you to bring back someone who isn't ordinary. Please tell Jake to come home. I know somehow you can deliver my message to him. Tell him to come home that I will tell him everything he needs to know, that life hasn't been the same ever since he left. Tell

Jake I'm cold and miserable," Lucinda pleaded. She then kept the seashell close to her bedside as she lay down and drifted off to sleep.

****

The following morning, Lucinda became restless. She barely touched her breakfast. Her Grandparents and parents tried to know what was wrong with her, but she dismissed the topic even before they brought it up.

"Where are you going to?" Greg asked as she saw Lucinda opening up the door.

"I'm going down the road to visit someone," Lucinda replied.

"The weather isn't too good. It's going to rain anytime. You should stay at home," Greg replied.

"Never mind. I'll be fine. Don't worry about me. I will be home soon," Lucinda replied.

"Is it Jake?" Greg asked.

"No," Lucinda replied as she swiftly left the house to avoid any more questions from her grandfather.

"Who was that?" Maya asked as soon as she came out.

"Oh, it's Lucinda. She said she was going out," Greg responded.

"It's going to rain anytime soon. I know Jake will bring her home safe," Maya added.

"She said she isn't going to visit Jake."

Maya interrogated. "Then who? She barely knows anyone else here. The only friend she has is just Anya and Jake. So, who is she going to visit?"

"When she comes home, you ask her that," Greg replied as he sat on the rocking chair.

It was already drizzling by the time Lucinda got to Jake's house. She sat on the balcony and directed her attention at the sky. It was a heavy downpour, but Lucinda sat still as the rain poured on her. To her, she wondered at the essence of going home. She needed the rain to heal this pain.

"You're going to get a cold," a familiar voice said as Lucinda turned to see Jake standing at the door.

Lucinda hurriedly stood up as she ran and hugged him tightly.

"Where did you go? I have been searching for you. I have come to this house every day, and I always sit here, waiting for you to see if you stroll down the street. I always looked out for you in the street, hoping to come home, but you never did. Please don't go, ever again," Lucinda said, crying.

Jake cleaned the tears off her face as he looked at her and said, "I'm never going away again. I will always be here with you."

Jake helped her inside as he brought out his towel so Lucinda could dry her body and her hair.

"You know you shouldn't have sat down there. It's raining heavily. You might get a cold," Jake asked.

"I always sit there," Lucinda said, pointing at her sitting point outside Jake's house. "That way, I can see people on the street; that way, I had hoped I would be able to see you when you're coming home. I'm glad you are home finally. Thank you for coming back," Lucinda replied.

"I'm happy to be back home. I missed everything here. Much more, I missed you." Jake said.

"Promise you will never leave again," Lucinda pleaded.

"I promise. This is still my home, so I'm not leaving soon," Jake responded. Lucinda smiled as she wrapped the towel around her body on hearing that.

"I told Anya that if you come back, I wouldn't hide my identity from you. Aside from being the girl who lost her parents a decade ago, I'm just like you, half-human, half-god. I was birthed by humans, though I won't say my mom is a full human. She is equally like me, but she didn't know till she died. She is literally from the moon and the stars. I'm Lucinda, the daughter of the moon and the stars, the heir to the throne. Anya isn't human. I guess you already know that. I didn't want to tell anyone because I didn't want what happened years back to happen again.

Everything about me has been kept in secrecy. I possess powers beyond human imagination, powers that I can't even control. I won't say I'm lucky, for being bestowed with all these comes with its challenges, happy and sad times.

This is Lucinda. This is everything about me. I know I should have told you earlier, but I wasn't sure if you would stay or not after hearing this. I was afraid that you might leave me if I should mention it to you. This was the reason I held back from telling you, not that I didn't trust you. I was just trying to protect myself," Lucinda explained.

"Thank you for telling me. I thought about coming back or staying back, but I felt we all deserved another chance. I realized what happened in your past life, how you were killed. I knew everything even before you told me. I just wanted you to tell me by yourself. I wanted you to trust me enough to confide in me about your identity," Jake responded.

"Then why did you leave? Why didn't you stay?" Lucinda asked.

"Because I wanted to fix a yawning bridge. I'm tired of seeing them at war. I want them to make peace with each other, and I left because I wanted to give you time to think about us," Jake replied.

"War? Who do you speak of?" Lucinda asked, surprised to hear this for the first time.

"Your mother and my father, the god, and goddess. They are enemies. Fate has assigned both of us to be together, but I'm still thinking if our union will make them become friends again. Sadly, I failed when I went home; they both detest each other," Jake replied.

"Fate? Are you the one fate has assigned to get married to me?" Lucinda asked. "I guess Anya or your mom didn't tell you about that. I found out, and I had to meet up with you. Perhaps, if I hadn't found out, none of them would have spoken to us about it," Jake replied.

"I see. Now it makes more sense. We will talk about this later," Lucinda said.

"Why? Are you scared of getting married?" Jake asked.

"I'm not scared of getting married. I just want you to follow me home. My grandparents have been asking about you. I need them to see you today at least. I lied to them for months. I would leave the house and tell them I'm coming to visit you. They have been asking me why I haven't been visiting, and I keep telling them soon. So, please let's go and visit them; at least I will be happy seeing that smile on their faces," Lucinda pleaded.

"Will you allow me to talk to your parents?" Jake asked.

"Sure, since you can see them," Lucinda said, smiling.

"And also, let's talk to your grandparents about us being soulmates. I know they will understand the need to know now. It's no use hiding it from them," Jake suggested.

"But don't you think it's early to let them know. They still see us as friends," Lucinda replied.

"I know. I guess you haven't told them about the real Jake. It would help if you told them everything. Look, Lucinda, we barely have enough time. You are turning 21 in less than five months. Anya should have told you all these. I guess she prevented you from doing anything with me," Jake implied.

"Anya knows," Lucinda asked with a shock on her face.

"Yes, she knows everything. I think that's why she tried painting me bad when we first met. I don't blame her. She has just been loyal to her queen. So, once we get there, we tell them, Lucinda, they deserve to know everything now," Jake replied.

Wow, I have been in the dark all this while. What more do I need to know?" Lucinda asked.

I don't know. Consult your book of prophecy. Ask your mom questions. They will answer," Jake replied.

"You know about the book of prophecy," Lucinda asked.

"Let's say I know everything that concerns you. You should know everything that concerns me. Don't worry. I will teach you everything you need to know," Jake replied, smiling.

Thank you," Lucinda replied.

"I guess the necklace is taking us there," Jake asked.

"You know so much about me," Lucinda said.

"Well, because I came out before you, and since you're my mate, I should know everything about who I'm spending my eternity with," Jake replied.

Lucinda smiled as they both stood up and held each other. Lucinda placed her hand on her necklace as they both disappeared from the room.

They both appeared in Lucinda's room. As they smiled at each other.

"You didn't tell me he was back," Anya said, sitting up from the bed as the duo turned to see Anya.

"Oh, you're here already," Lucinda said.

"Yes, welcome home, Prince Jake," Anya said.

Jake walked closer to the bed as he took the seashell and walked closer to Lucinda.

"I got the message. Jake delivered the message just the way you said it, more reason I came back home. I wouldn't want to steal the shine I brought to your life," Jake said as Lucinda smiled and hugged him.

"It's still raining. After meeting your grandparents and parents, will you take me home?" Jake asked.

"You can sleep here, right?" Lucinda asked.

"What happens to me? Where will I sleep?" Anya blurted out.

"You see," Jake said.

"Anya, not like you sleep here all the time," Lucinda said.

"I know, but I want to sleep here tonight," Anya replied.

"You can go to my house," Jake chipped in as Anya looked at him and lay back on the bed.

"Let's go," Lucinda said as she dragged Jake out of the room. Greg and Maya were shocked to see Jake with Lucinda.

"We have been sitting here for a few hours. How and when did you both gain entrance to the house?" Greg asked.

"My usual stuff," Lucinda replied as Maya stood up and hugged Jake tightly.

"We missed you," Maya said, smiling.

"Same here. I'm sorry I didn't stop by all this time," Jake apologized.

"We are good. I'm happy you're here with us," Greg responded.

Jake sat down with Lucinda as he slowly said to her," Is it okay to call your parents mom and dad?"

"Sure, you can," Lucinda replied, as Greg and Maya looked at them.

"What's going on?" Greg asked.

"Can he see us?" Phil asked.

"Yes, I can see you both. I'm just like your daughter," Jake replied.

"Lucinda, what did you do?" Annalise asked, puzzled.

"I didn't do anything. The truth is, Jake is like me," Lucinda replied.

"How do you mean?" Maya asked.

"I'm just like her. She is from the moon and the stars, and I'm the son of the sun. I knew who she was even before we became friends, and I saw your ghost each time I visited, but I couldn't talk about it. I'm just like your daughter, and I want to be seen as Jake," Jake replied.

"Wow! This is hard to believe." Greg said.

"I thought you were human like us," Maya added.

"I'm still human. I was born by earthly parents," Jake replied.

"Dad, mom, grandpa, and Grandma, I need to tell you something, Jake and I are mates," Lucinda said.

"I don't understand," Maya said.

"It means they are husband and wife, more like destined to end up with each other," Anya yelled out as she came out of the room.

"Lucinda, is she joking or serious?" Phil asked.

"I know Lucinda has a better explanation," Annalise added.

"You aren't saying anything?" Maya said, looking at Lucinda.

"You all should calm down and let her explain. Jake is a good man, and Lucinda is in perfect hands if they bother to end up together. So, allow them to talk," Greg said.

"The truth is that even before we were born, it has been pre-destined that we will end up with each other. Our parents didn't say a word to us because of their hostility. I got to know the truth, and I had to search for Lucinda and luckily, she was in the same town as me.

Our spirits aligned immediately. We got to meet each other that day. Fate has it that our marriage will reunite the two worlds, and I know that's true. Aside from the prophecy talking about us, even if fate hadn't said anything, I would have still ended up with Lucinda. I love her. Life makes sense to her. I wouldn't want to throw away what we have," Jake explained.

"And they need to get married before Lucinda turns 21. You both are getting married soon," came in Anya.

"You knew about it all," Lucinda asked, surprised at Anya's words.

"Yeah, but it wasn't my power to talk to you about it. Now you know, let me tell you the truth you need to know. You have to get married before the next full moon," Anya replied as she walked inside the room.

"I thought she would stay with us a few more years," Maya stammered.

"Same here. It's so soon. Lucinda can't leave us now," Greg half protested.

"Even if I marry Jake, his house is just a stone's throw. This is my home. I will always visit. My family lives here, and I'm from here. I can't forget home," Lucinda assured.

"My daughter has grown. I thought you were the same Lucinda we left ten years ago." Phil added.

"I wish you would stay a few more years; I just wish," Annalise said.

"This is home. I'm still going to come around. You all are making me cry. No one is taking my room. Even if I turn Jake's wife tomorrow, I'm still your daughter, and I'm still your grandchild," Lucinda said with a teary voice as Maya stood up and hugged her tightly.

"I know she will be safe with you," Phil said.

"I swear by my throne. Nothing shall hurt Lucinda," Jake replied.

****

They had a small wedding strictly at 12:30 am, after which Lucinda wanted to hug her parents, Annalise and Phil, before leaving for Jake's house. Maya and Greg were happy, but the tears couldn't let them say a word. They knew that Lucinda would go, but they didn't think it would be soon.

Maya and Annalise hugged Lucinda tightly after the marriage vows were taken.

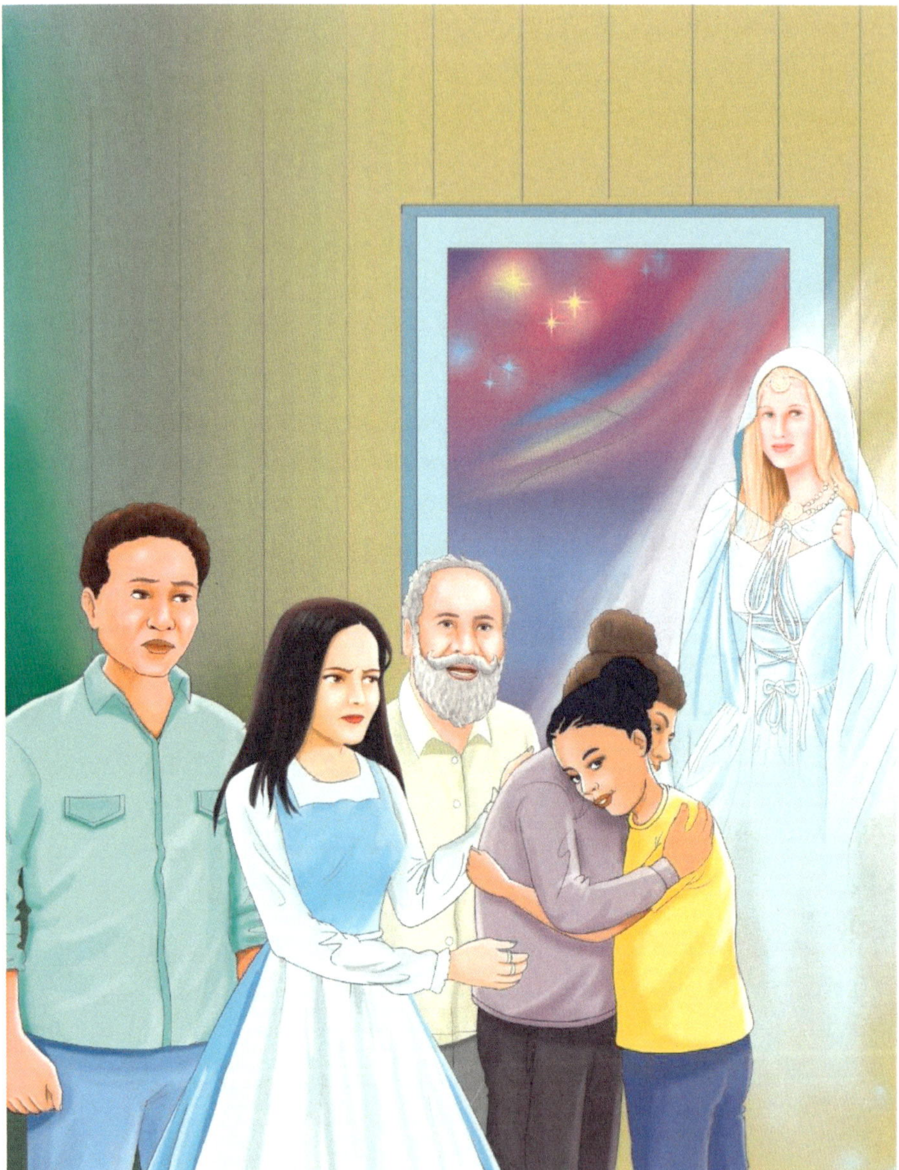

"Please come back by morning. We want to have breakfast with you and Jake," Maya pleaded.

"Please, Lucinda, don't say no," Annalise added.

"I will be here; I promise," Lucinda said.

"Or we will get to spend the remaining days here. If we visit tomorrow morning, we won't leave till next week," Jake chipped in.

"That's a nice idea," Greg said.

"Thank you so much. I love you and Jake. I know you both will enjoy everything life denied us," Phil prayed.

Lucinda smiled as she hugged her father. She then took turns in embracing his family. On getting to Anya's turn, she said, "You know where to find me. You will always visit, right."

"You know I will. You're my assignment here on earth," Anya smiled as she hugged Lucinda tightly.

Lucinda held her husband as they both bade farewell to all of them before disappearing from the house.

They appeared in Jake's house as Jake wiped the tears off Lucinda's face. It was apparent she was already missing her family. It was already late. They had to go straight to bed.

Lucinda lay on the bed as he watched Jake flip through the book of prophecy.

"How long have you had this?" Jake asked.

"For some time, it came at the right time," Lucinda replied.

"Your grandparents are super excited that we bought this. They have grown so addicted to you. At some point, I thought they wouldn't let you get married, but I'm glad it's all over now. We are couples, and we still live close to them," Jake said.

"Yeah, I wish Amber was here too. I wish she were around to witness all these. I still can't believe that she is gone," Lucinda said.

"I have this strong feeling that she will come home soon. She isn't like you, and neither is she like Anya. Her time here on earth was limited. She came for a purpose, and that purpose was you, and she is through with it. You have to live every day with smiles on your face, knowing that she will come back someday," Jake responded.

"Thank You," Lucinda said, smiling.

Jake stood up as he dropped the book of prophecy on the shelf. He then came back and lay close to Lucinda.

"The world ordained our marriage even before we were born. We will make a perfect couple and bridge the gap between the moon and the sun," Jake said.

"I hope we break the enmity between those two," Lucinda said.

"Do you think our adventure here on earth is over?" Lucinda asked.

"I don't know, but the truth is, I don't think it's over. We are not mortals, so definitely, problems will come for us to solve them.

We were assigned to this world on purpose, but I know whatever will come won't be bigger than us," Jake replied.

"Thank you for coming back," Lucinda said, smiling.

"I can't be mad at you for long. I love and value what we have," Jake replied.

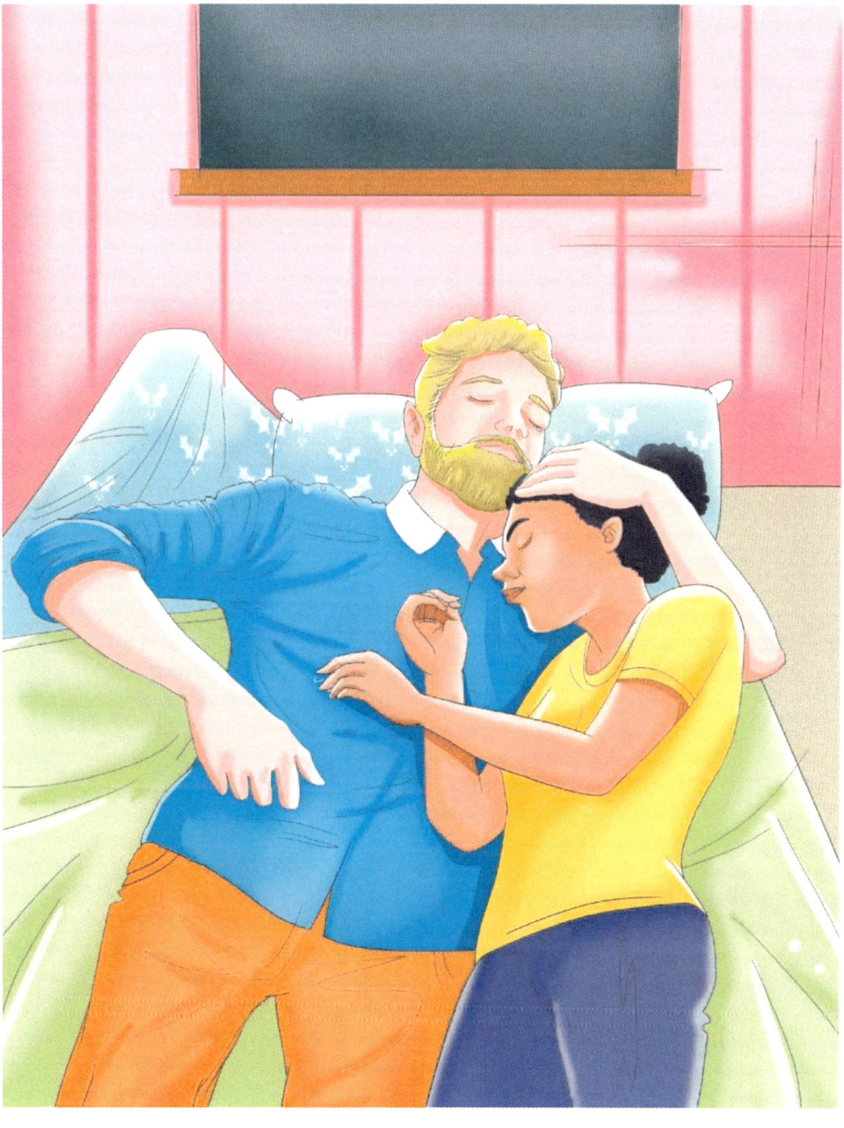

◆ ◆ ◆

CHAPTER ELEVEN

"Lucinda, come and see this," Jake beckoned to Lucinda, who swiftly dropped the bag she was holding.

Jake handed the Book of Prophecy to her, showing her a page with an image glowing.

"Has this been here all the time?" Lucinda asked, surprised.

"No, the book suddenly glowed on its own, which made me pick it up, and that was when I saw a new message appear," Jake replied.

"This is huge. I don't even know if I'm ready to go through this stress again. Our marriage is just five months old. I don't want to be tasked with this," Lucinda replied mournfully.

"I understand if you don't want to go through this, but it will be fun doing this with you, saving the world together," Jake replied.

"This monster; I just can't deal ... but wait, something looks familiar here," Lucinda said as she ran her hands on the book.

"The man bears the image of a star," Lucinda observed.

"Have you encountered him before?" Jake asked.

"No, but something seems odd. I'm trying to place my hand on it. Seeing the star on the body, why can't I fix this simple riddle?" Lucinda shouted.

"You have to take it easy. Sit and think. By so, you might be able to solve the riddle," Jake replied as Lucinda sighed and sat down on the chair.

"The mark on the body looks familiar. I'm trying to recollect something," Lucinda said.

"You mean the star?" Jake asked.

"Yes, the star," Lucinda answered.

"Okay, I know you will remember sooner or later, but don't worry about it. You don't have to kill yourself about it. The main issue is how to take him out of the picture and send him to the beyond so he can never bother the world again," Jake replied.

"Why can't they just quit? Why do they keep coming back? And, why should we be the ones to protect the world, putting our lives on the line?" Lucinda asked.

"We are gods. We are special and sent here for a reason. Demons feel they have been living in the shadow of humans for so long. Since humans have no powers, they should not be allowed to stay and rule the earth. Hopefully, someday the world and the world beyond will be erased of all the demons," Jake replied.

"I just hope so," Lucinda replied as she stood up and walked into the room.

Jake took the book as he read through the content of the "**Book of Prophecy."**

Lucinda walked into the bedroom to see Anya standing close to the window.

"Anya, you're here," Lucinda said as she quickly hugged her.

"Sagar is out. I guess he came to see if he could complete the things other demons couldn't do," Anya said.

"Do you mean the demon which appeared in the Book of Prophecy?" Lucinda asked.

"Yes."

"Wait. How did you find out?" Lucinda asked.

"Lucinda, I'm a spirit. I have lived for centuries, so I can sense whenever evil lurks. I'm a beast too. So, I can sense when demons are around," Anya replied.

"That's true. I almost forgot. I'm already getting used to seeing you as a human that I forgot who you are," Lucinda said as she sat on the bed.

'I'm just scared. I'm angry too," Anya said, still leaning on the wall.

"Is there any problem? You know you can always talk to me," Lucinda said.

"Of course, it's about **Asgard**.

I can't go with you on this one. I'm angry that I won't be part of some of your adventures to save humanity. I'm scared that something bad might happen to you. I'm scared that Asgard might try to hurt you," Anya said.

"***You're a beast.***

You shouldn't be scared. Things like this shouldn't weigh you down, but why can't you go with me? Is there any reason for that? Any restrictions? You know I can talk to the queen, and she will allow you," Lucinda said.

"No, the rules were made even before your mother started reigning. Since you're now married, you and your husband will undertake any adventure. It can only be in rare cases that I will be permitted to go with you. I'm just tensed. I do not want anything to happen to you. I know you're a goddess, but Lucinda, this part of you is still human," Anya moaned.

"Yeah, you're right. This part of me is still human. I have emotions to start with. If I can change the rules, you know I will, but I need you to do something for me when I'm away with Jake," Lucinda asked.

"You know you don't need to ask. Just tell me what you want, and I will do it right away," Anya said.

"Protect my parents and my grandparents, and don't let them know about this adventure we are about to undertake. I will come to visit before we leave, but whatever happens, protect them all and my horses. Please take good care of them. They are still my family," Lucinda pleaded.

"They are my family too. I will protect them with the last drop of my blood. That's a promise," Anya replied.

"Thank you so much, Anya. I don't know what I would have done without you. Thank you for standing with me all these years, but I'm still pleading. Please don't disappear from me again. I don't want to wake up one morning looking for you," Lucinda pleaded.

"No, I won't disappear from you. I'm here to stay for as long as you want me to stay," Anya replied.

"Thank you so much," Lucinda said as she stood up and hugged Anya tightly.

"Send my greetings to Jake," Anya said as she bade Lucinda goodbye before disappearing.

Lucinda took the seashell as she sat down on the bed. Then, the door flung open as Jake walked in.

"Anya here," Jake asked as he dropped the book of prophecy on the shelf.

"How did you know?" Lucinda asked, smiling.

"I'm a god. I can sense and feel everything. Guess she was here to tell you she won't be going with you," Jake asked as he sat down close to Lucinda.

"Jake!" Lucinda asked with her eyes wide open.

"Anya is a beast. She senses when **demons are coming**.

I don't know how it feels like waking up one morning and being told you can't do things with someone you have always done things with. I wish somehow that some rules will be changed," Jake said.

"You know more than I do. I will change some rules when I get to that position," Lucinda replied.

"Your reign is coming with new things, I guess," Jake asked.

"Exactly," Lucinda replied, smiling.

"We will visit my parents and grandparents, but we are not telling them about this adventure. We are just telling them that we are going on a trip. I don't want them getting worked up for anything. We have to come back for them," Lucinda said, betraying a wry smile.

"I will make sure of that. We will come back. That's a promise," Jake assured.

" I know I have the best husband in the whole world. I'm lucky to have ended up with you," Lucinda said.

"I couldn't thank the universe more for making us mates," Jake said as he slowly hugged Lucinda.

****

Jake and Lucinda got to the door and knocked.

"They will be happy to see us," Jake said.

"And also angry with me that I haven't visited for a while now," Lucinda replied.

The door opened to see Anya standing there as she hugged

Lucinda.

You didn't tell me you were coming here. I was with you a few days ago," Anya said.

"Who is at the door?" Maya asked, coming towards the entrance door to see for herself.

As soon as she saw Lucinda, she shouted and hugged her. After which, they all walked inside and sat down while Maya clung to her granddaughter.

"I missed my baby," Maya said.

"I'm an adult, Grandma," Lucinda said, smiling.

"And our baby, you will always be," Greg said, smiling as he hugged Jake.

"I'm happy you both came to visit today," Maya said.

"Yeah, we came to know how you're doing, but where are my parents?" Lucinda asked, looking around.

"Oh, they are not here at the moment, but I think they will soon be back," Greg replied

"Jake, you're doing a wonderful job taking care of our girl," Maya said.

"If I don't take care of her, I would have failed," Jake replied, smiling.

"Grandma and Grandpa, I want to talk to you about something important," Lucinda said.

"Is there any problem?" Maya asked.

"You know we will always do anything for you two," Greg added.

"We want to go on a trip for just a week, and we will come home," Lucinda replied slowly.

"It's important; you have to let them go," Anya added.

Maya and Greg looked at each other and nodded, but sadness was written all over their faces. Though they weren't living together anymore, they felt this uneasiness whenever they were to be separated from Lucinda, even for a moment.

"I promise. We will spend a week here once we are back," Jake added.

"Is that a promise?" Maya asked.

"Yes, it's a promise," Lucinda said, smiling as she hugged Maya.

Jake and Greg stood up and left the sitting room for the garden.

****

The giant figure opened its eyes, revealing its purple eyes, smiling as he walked closer to the mirror to touch it.

"You know they might kill you. You just leave," one of the demons said.

"Yes, they might kill me, but that isn't certain. How long will they remain powerful to wipe out all the demons in this world? After me, another will come, and more will still come."

"So, you think they will quit and hand over the world to you?" The other demon asked.

"They have to, Elyon. They have to. This world is ours. It has always been ours. Humans can't come out and take over," Asgard shouted.

"Maybe you shouldn't have unveiled yourself right now. These tricks won't take you anywhere far. They will still defeat you," Elyon said.

"And when they do that, you all shouldn't stop fighting. Somehow the world will become ours. Someone in our midst has to make us proud," Asgard replied.

"Okay, your wish is our command," Elyon said as he bowed and left the place.

Asgard touched the mirror and smiled as Lucinda and Jake appeared in the mirror.

"Oh, it seems they are coming already, making it easier. I don't have to leave here. They will come to meet me," Asgard said, smiling.

"I hope you both have bid your final goodbye to people who mean a lot to you? Even if I don't take you both out today, someone else will. This world is ours. It's just a matter of time for the house owner to get back home. I must have my revenge," Asgard said, tightening his fist. Next, he screamed out loud, which made Elyon appear back, "you called?" Elyon said.

"Take them out. Hide them far away from where they can't be seen. You all have to leave now," Asgard commanded.

"And what about you?" Elyon asked.

"I will be fine," Asgard replied.

"You know that's not true. You need us just as we need you. What will happen to you? You can't fight this on your own. Better still, let's leave them. We are okay where we are. No matter how hard we try, we won't win this fight. Star didn't win it, and "

"Don't you dare talk about my mother in that manner," Asgard shouted, cutting Elyon off?

"She was hibernating, which made it easier for them to kill her," Asgard added.

"Then, how many more will we lose fighting over a lost battle? Asgard looks around. We are okay here. Lucinda and Jake are joined together, making it ten times more difficult to hurt them. They were sent to earth for a reason. They possess powers that they don't even know of, greater than ours. They are special," Elyon countered.

"They are not special. We are the ones. They are gods. It doesn't mean they can't be killed," Asgard shouted.

"We are special too, but the truth has been told. We can't kill them. They can only kill themselves," Elyon replied.

"I don't want to hear anything else. Leave now," Asgard commanded, but Elyon would have none of that.

"Asgard, we can live peacefully with them. We can stop this war and end all this. Creating war where there is none means we will lose our abode just for this. Why are you being so desperate?" Elyon asked as Asgard threw a slap at him.

"Leave. Take them away from here. If I don't come back, make a home there and groom someone else. This fight has to continue. We must redeem what is ours," Asgard shouted.

Elyon bowed as he quickly left the place. Asgard placed his hands on the metal lying on the floor as he muttered some strange words, making the metal dissolve into dust.

Asgard drew his strength from the metal. He needed metal to stay alive and strong.

"I'm not fighting a lost battle. Mother needs to get her revenge.

They have ruled for a long time, but now is the time for demons to take over. We can't keep living in the shadow of humans. It's now or never," Asgard whispered as he disappeared immediately.

****

Lucinda and Jake walked out of the lightning portal and looked around to see where they were.

"This place looks deserted," Jake said.

"I know, and I can feel this negativity hovering around here," Lucinda said.

"Let's go. I believe what we came for is somewhere around here," Jake said as Lucinda nodded, and they both walked away.

"I think we need to get closer to those pillars. Something is lurking around there," Lucinda said as Jake agreed.

Asgard smiled as he saw Lucinda and Jake approaching.

"You didn't wait for me to come. You came looking for me instead," Asgard said, laughing.

"So, should we wait till you bring ruin to the world before we stop you? We can't. What do you want? You know you can leave, and we won't hurt you," Jake added.

"Hurt me? I'm not weak like my mother. I waited patiently for this day. Now I will have my revenge. I'm sorry that you won't only be losing your wife, you will also be losing your unborn child," Asgard said as he stood up to his full length.

Lucinda touched her stomach as she looked at Jake.

"Leave here; go," Jake whispered.

If it had occurred to Jake that Lucinda was pregnant, he wouldn't have gone on this journey with her.

"No, I can't leave you here. Yes, he might hurt us, but he definitely can't kill us. We possess way more powers than he," Lucinda replied.

"Asgard, when you speak of your mother, who is she? Was she that weak? I had to take her off this world permanently," Lucinda asked as Asgard growled?

"Don't you dare speak of my mother like that," Asgard shouted.

"She was weak. Why are you hurt? You're just a piece of cake when Lucinda can easily do away with your mother," Jake said as Asgard spat out a burning ball filled with sulfur.

Asgard was surprised to see Jake standing with no bruises on his body on impact with the burning sulfur.

"Let me remind you again who I am. I'm Jake, the son of the sun. I am fire itself. You can't fight me with fire," Jake replied.

"Then I will fight you with your enemy," Asgard said.

When he was about to evoke water by the side, a strong wind

pinned him on the wall as Lucinda advanced and shouted, "I control the wind, water, and this earth. Everything bows at my feet, Asgard. I don't want to hurt you. Leave and never come back," Lucinda shouted as lightning struck, followed by the rumbling of the thunder.

"It was easy for you to defeat her because she was hibernating. Do you think I'm a weakling?" Asgard shouted.

"Oh, that makes more sense. Star is your mother. I knew something familiar about you, and you explained it. So, Star was your mother. I didn't hurt her. I only chose to end things peacefully for her. I didn't even inflict the right pain on her. She came for my parents, which was her greatest mistake." Lucinda shouted back. "I would have hurt your grandparents if I was her," Asgard replied as Jake evoked the rock there, and it came crashing down on Asgard's face.

"Speak one more word about our family, and I will ruin you," Jake threatened with his tightened fist.

Asgard lay on the floor as he muttered some strange words, and everything started visibly shaking as Lucinda and Jake held each other tightly.

"Don't even try because you can't stop this. The earth will swallow you up. I will make your death an easy one, and after that, I will have the freedom to do all I wish," Asgard said, laughing.

"Are you that desperate?" Lucinda asked.

"Yes, I'm desperate to bring doom and damnation to the world just like my mother wanted. She will be so proud of me," Asgard said, laughing.

"Lucinda concentrates. I know you can. Let's do this," Jake said.

"I can't. The ground is shaking. I'm trying to hold my balance," Lucinda replied. "Speak to the winds. They will hear you," Jake whispered.

Lucinda closed her eyes to mutter some words, but she opened them immediately as she whispered, "I'm sorry, I just can't concentrate,"

"Okay, just hold on to me," Jake said as he made a strange drawing on the floor while muttering some unfamiliar words.

"What did you do?" Lucinda asked.

"I summoned our parents. I'm not saying we are weak, but we can barely concentrate. Maybe when we are out of here, we can work on our balance," Jake said.

The shape of the moon and stars together with the sun appeared, and the light was so blinding that they didn't see what happened next.

Lucinda and Jake opened their eyes to see a staff right in their hands.

"You summoned the Queen and the King? What makes you think they possess human attributes like you to appear here? How dare you involve them in a party they weren't invited to. You both are fighting a lost battle. Your parents can't help," Asgard said, laughing. Jake and Lucinda joined their staff together as they enchanted some words together.

"Go home. Damnation can't be brought to the world now," they both uttered as the light from the staff fired straight at Asgard.

They both closed their eyes and fell to the floor from the ensuing explosion.

Lucinda and Jake opened their eyes to see everywhere around were ruined by the explosion.

Jake helped Lucinda up as they strolled to where Asgard was lying down, coughing.

"I know it's over for me. You have sent me where you sent my mother, Star. You both pulled a strong fight. You might have won, but unforeseen demons will always come around. The fight hasn't ended. We demons still exist," Asgard said, laughing as he slowly faded into thin air, leaving some flowers on the floor.

"The staff, where are they?" Lucinda asked, looking around.

"They are gone and belong to our parents. Asgard was right. We can't make them appear here. They have a place solely designed for them. Let's just say their spirits took over our bodies. They have done their bidding and returned to their palaces," Jake replied.

"How? Who am I married to?" Lucinda asked.

"You have a lot to learn, and I will teach you everything," Jake replied.

"Let's go home then," Lucinda said.

Jake bent down as he kissed Lucinda's stomach and said, "I'm so sorry I brought you out to experience this. If I knew you were in momma's womb, I wouldn't have stressed you. Daddy is so sorry. I can hardly wait to meet you."

"Funny enough, a demon told us we will be parents. I will tell my daughter how her presence was announced to us," Lucinda said, laughing.

"Daughter? You seem so sure," Jake asked.

"Yeah, Amber is coming back. She promised that she would come back as our first child, so I believe I will give birth to her," Lucinda said.

"Nice, is a seer, daughter of the moon and the stars, and also the daughter of the sun. How lucky can she be?" Jake replied, laughing back.

"Very lucky. We will stay alive for her," Lucinda added.

"Let's go home," Jake said as Lucinda touched her necklace, opening the portal before they both walked in.

◆ ◆ ◆

CHAPTER TWELVE

Lucinda lay on the bed, her hand gripping Jake tightly as waves of pain and anticipation washed over her. The room echoed with the rhythm of her breaths, the moments stretching into eternity. With a final push, the cries of a newborn filled the air, and Lucinda's heart swelled with overwhelming love and relief.

As the town nurse placed the bundle of joy in Lucinda's arms, tears welled up in her eyes. She gazed down at her daughter, a radiant warmth flooding her being. "Amber," she whispered, her voice filled with tenderness, knowing this name held a significance that transcended the ordinary. She promised that she would name her child after Amber, the seer. Lucinda couldn't help but notice the subtle yet striking similarities between her daughter and Amber. From the curve of her smile to the sparkle in her eyes, an uncanny resemblance went beyond mere genetics. It felt like Amber returned to this world for the second time.

One evening, sitting with her husband Jake in the warmth of their home, Lucinda couldn't contain her observations any longer. "Jake," she began, her voice tinged with curiosity, "have you noticed how much our daughter resembles Amber?"
Jake nodded, a smile playing on his lips. "It's almost uncanny sometimes," he replied, his eyes reflecting his affection for his wife and daughter.

Lucinda pondered the resemblance, a mix of wonder and intrigue dancing in her thoughts. She traced the contours of Amber's face in her mind; the familiarity of Amber the seer features an unspoken connection between them. It was as if her daughter carried a reflection of Amber's essence, proof of the bond they shared.

"Remember Amber's prophecy?" Jake leaned back, a playful smile tugging at the corners of his lips.

Lucinda's eyes sparkled with curiosity. "Oh, you mean her claim about coming back as our child?" she chuckled softly. "Yes, she did promise that, and it's obvious she kept her promise. For once, I thought I was never going to see her again.

Jake nodded, a thoughtful expression crossing his face. "It's intriguing. The idea of her returning in a different form, possibly with powers or abilities we can't fathom."

Lucinda leaned in with her gaze fixed on Jake. "But what kind of powers could she possess? Will she be a free spirit, a wanderer between worlds?" I'm scared, Jake, even if I don't say it. I don't want my child to go through half of what I went through here on earth, discovering who I am and the battles I had to fight."

Jake's smile widened; his eyes filled with assurance. "Whatever powers she may possess, whatever form she takes, I'm certain of one thing: the convergence of our worlds, the ones she comes from, won't bring trouble upon our path. Trust me, she won't go through any of what you went through. Do you know why? Because you have cleared the path for her, that which she will be grateful for in years to come."

Lucinda sighed, a mix of wonder and apprehension evident in her voice. "It's just the unknown, Jake. The unpredictability of it all, I want what's best for her and everybody."

"I understand, love." Jake reached out and gently grasped Lucinda's hand. "But Amber has always been a beacon of positivity, a guide through uncertainty. She's not the kind to bring chaos but rather happiness. Her past life may not be easy, but her present life with us as her parents will be the easiest for her."

Lucinda's gaze softened, a sense of trust enveloping her. "You're right. She's always been an embodiment of wisdom and balance."

As they sat in contemplative silence, memories of their encounters with Amber flooded their minds. Her serene presence, her cryptic yet reassuring words echoed in their thoughts, a being who was blessed beyond measure.

"We might never truly comprehend the extent of her abilities," Lucinda mused. "But I hope she brings the same warmth and kindness she always exuded."

"I couldn't agree more," Jake nodded in agreement. "Her presence has always been a blessing, a beacon of hope in our lives."

****

As Greg and Maya entered the house, Lucinda greeted them warmly, embracing them tightly. Their eyes sparkled with excitement, eager to see their great-grandchild, Amber. Lucinda pointed towards Amber's room, understanding their intent, and they hurried off to be with her.

Alone in the room with Amber, the atmosphere was filled with a sense of innocent curiosity. Amber looked up at her great-grandparents with curious eyes and asked, "Why don't Grandma Annalise and Grandpa Phil play or hug me? Did I do anything wrong?"

Maya was momentarily taken aback by the unexpected question, unsure how to respond, while Greg leaned closer to Amber, trying to find the right words. "Sweetheart, they're not angry with you, and you didn't do anything wrong, okay? They're different; sometimes they can't play or hug like we do."

Amber's face scrunched up in confusion. "But I want to hug them. Can you ask them, please?" she pleaded, her innocence tugging at Greg's heartstrings.

Greg's eyes softened with empathy. "I know you want to, and they want to hug you too. But it might take some time. They're not mad, I promise."

Maya, touched by Amber's yearning, finally found her voice. "Amber, Grandma Annalise, and Grandpa Phil love you very much. They watch over you, even if they can't hug or play right now."

Amber's little face lit up with a hint of understanding. "Okay," she said, a small smile on her lips.

Greg scooped Amber into a warm embrace, trying to reassure her. "We'll all play together soon, alright?"

Amber nodded, her eyes brightening with anticipation. "Okay, Grandpa," she said, giggling as Maya joined in with a playful tickle.

Greg and Maya engaged Amber in games and playful activities throughout the day. The moments were filled with laughter and joy. Amber's innocent question lingered in the air, a reminder of the gentle patience required to bridge the gap between her and her ghostly grandparents, Annalise and Phil.

That evening, when Greg and Maya left for their home, it didn't last long for Jake and Amber to disappear into the quiet evening for their stroll. A subtle shift in the atmosphere settled over the house.

Later that night, the midnight stillness was interrupted by Jake's gentle touch as he woke Lucinda, concern etched on his face. "Lucinda, wake up," he whispered urgently, his voice filled with wonder.

Blinking away the remnants of sleep, Lucinda rubbed her eyes, a mix of confusion and concern on her face. "Is everything okay?" she asked, her voice laced with sleepiness.

Jake embraced her tenderly, guiding her gently towards Amber's room. "Come, you have to see this," he said softly, his eyes glinting with excitement and awe.

Confused but trusting Jake's lead, Lucinda followed him into Amber's room. As they stepped inside, a breathtaking sight unfolded before them. The two-year-old lay peacefully, surrounded by a celestial spectacle. Stars danced around her, and sunlight seemed to orbit her, creating a mesmerizing display that defied explanation.

Lucinda gasped in awe, her hand covering her mouth in disbelief. "What... ho ..." Her words trailed off, unable to comprehend the ethereal sight before her.

A radiant smile graced Jake's lips as he held Lucinda closer, his eyes fixed on their remarkable child. "Our parents came to visit their grandchild," he said, his voice filled with wonder and pride.

Lucinda's heart swelled with mixed emotions - wonder, joy, and a sense of connection. Tears of awe welled in her eyes as she gazed upon the extraordinary scene, realizing the importancc of their daughter's unique lineage.

She stepped closer to Amber, a sense of reverence washing over her.

"She truly is something special," Lucinda whispered, her voice filled with an inexplicable sense of pride and love.

Sitting together on the bed, they whispered about the strange occurrence. "Do you think we did it? Bridged the gap between worlds?" Lucinda asked, her voice tinged with curiosity.

The events of the evening left them feeling amazed and intrigued. Thoughts whirled in their minds as they dozed off, wondering what this newfound link between worlds might mean for their future and the future of their child, Amber. But whatever it was, they were sure they would handle it.

As Amber celebrated her third birthday, Lucinda observed something extraordinary about her daughter—subtle manifestations of supernatural abilities that seemed to emanate from within her. Objects occasionally levitated when Amber was excited. She communicated effortlessly with animals, giggles attracting butterflies and birds wherever she played.

Lucinda, having harbored her abilities, recognized the signs immediately. Rather than being alarmed, she found solace in realizing that Amber had inherited these extraordinary gifts from herself and Jake.

One sunny afternoon in the backyard, Lucinda watched Amber hold out her tiny hand, her eyes sparkling with innocent curiosity. A small sapling struggling to grow suddenly sprouted leaves, blooming with vibrant flowers as Amber's laughter filled the air.

While witnessing the scene, Jake approached Lucinda, his expression a mix of wonder and understanding. "She's like us, isn't she?" he remarked softly, his eyes fixed on their daughter.

Lucinda nodded, a gentle smile gracing her lips. "Yes, she is our little miracle, carrying the wonders of something beyond the ordinary. We're lucky to have her."

Embracing their daughter's unique abilities, Lucinda and Jake nurtured Amber's burgeoning powers, guiding her with love and care. They knew that within her lay a potential that transcended the bounds of the ordinary. A gift that, when honed and understood, could become a beacon of hope, and wonder in a world filled with mysteries yet to be explored.

****

Amber, her little feet padding softly on the floor, approached her parents, a furrow forming on her brow as she reached out to touch them. "Mommy, Daddy, why can't I hug Grandma Annalise and Grandpa Phil as I do with Big Grandpa Greg and Grandma Maya?"

Jake and Lucinda exchanged glances. Their hearts softened by Amber's innocence. Jake crouched down, meeting her curious gaze. "Sweetheart, it's not that they don't want to hug you. It's just that they can't."

Amber's eyes widened. "Why not? Don't they like me?"

Lucinda kneeled beside her, wrapping her arms around Amber. "Of course they do, darling. They have a special way of being here."

"How?" Amber's voice carried a hint of confusion.

"Your grandparents turn into something called ghosts during the day," Lucinda explained gently.

"Ghosts?" Amber's voice quivered slightly.

Jake nodded, trying to find the most straightforward words. "Yes, they're like spirits, sweetie. People who have left this world."

"But why are they here if they're gone?" Amber's innocence begged for understanding.

Lucinda smiled softly, tracing a finger along Amber's cheek. "You see, honey, Mommy and Daddy are different. I come from the moon and stars, and your daddy comes from the Sun. So, some things work differently for us."

Amber blinked, trying to make sense of the magical explanation. "Who am I then?"

Lucinda's eyes twinkled with affection. "You, my dear, are something special. With time, you'll discover who you truly are."

Feeling curious and fascinated, Amber took her parents' hands as they led her back to her room. They tucked her in, showering her with kisses, and left her to drift into the realm of dreams, unaware of the enchanting encounters awaiting her as the clock struck midnight.

The clock's chime pierced the silence of Amber's room as midnight arrived. Annalise and Phil, the spectral forms of her grandparents, appeared, their translucent figures casting a soft glow in the dimly lit room. With a tender longing, Annalise extended her hand towards Amber, intending to stroke her hair as she slept.

"Grandma! Grandpa!" Amber's voice filled with excitement.

Surprised, Annalise asked, "My dear, why are you awake late?"

Giggling with innocence, Amber sat up. "I was waiting for you!"

Phil couldn't help but chuckle at her sincerity. "You were waiting for us?"

"Yep!" Amber affirmed, enveloping her grandparents in a heartfelt embrace. "Someone told me that if I want to hug you, then I have to wait until midnight; she is right,"

"And who is that," Annalise asked.

"It's my secret; I promised her I wouldn't tell anyone about her. "Have you been coming every night?" Amber asked smiling

A tender warmth enveloped Annalise and Phil at Amber's innocent inquiry. "Yes, darling, we have," Annalise replied, her voice filled with affection.

Happiness flashed across Amber's face as she nestled back onto her pillow. "Don't worry, I'll find a way so you don't have to wait till midnight to play with me again, and Mommy doesn't have to wait till midnight to hug you both."

Annalise and Phil exchanged glances, a shimmer of hope reflecting in their translucent forms. Their heart swelled with gratitude for the unwavering love of their grandchild, even though they both knew it wasn't possible. Lucinda had already done what her powers could do.

Amber closed her eyes with a comforting smile, her breathing becoming steady and calm as sleep gently reclaimed her. Annalize and Phil watched over her for a moment. Ensuring she was deeply asleep, they reappeared in the familiar surroundings of their parent's home before slowly fading away from her room.

Greg and Maya were overjoyed to see their daughter and son-in-law, the ethereal reunion filling the room with warmth and love. Conversations flowed effortlessly, recounting tales of the past and sharing glimpses of their unseen world.

Greg bid them goodnight as the night deepened, his heart full from the brief yet cherished encounter. It didn't take long before Maya bid them goodnight. Annalise and Phil sat on the balcony and watched the stars and the moon that night.

"What Amber said will hurt when she realizes she can't do anything. She is such a sweet little child," Annalise said, breaking the silence.

Phil chuckled and said, "She will grow to understand the realities of life."

"The truth is, I'm happy that Lucinda and Jake aren't fully human. Laying on the deathbed and thinking about my child was the worst thing ever. I fought death. I wanted to stay alive for my baby, but I guess I didn't fight enough. I watched my daughter go through hell, even though my parents were taking good care of her. All she wanted was her parents. I'm happy that whatever happens, Amber won't have to go through the same thing Lucinda went through. She won't bear the same scar that our death caused to her daughter," Annalise uttered as Phil shifted closer to her and hugged her tightly.

Phil smiled as he looked at the Stars. "I'm happy that things turned out well for Lucinda. It would help if you were happy, too. We got the chance that many never got."

****

Alone in the dimly lit room, Lucinda gazed at the night sky through the window, the stars twinkling like distant whispers. She couldn't shake off the unease about her daughter's future and the unknown path ahead.

With a heavy heart, Lucinda whispered into the silent room, Lucinda stood up as she walked into her room. Jake was fast asleep already. She lay down on the bed, staring into blank space. Thoughts of Amber and the complexities of being a mother swirled through Lucinda's mind. The soft glow of the moonlight seeped into the room, casting shadows that seemed to mirror the uncertainty she felt.

Despite the tranquility of the night, Lucinda's heart remained restless, haunted by the unspoken worries about her beloved daughter. The night went on, leaving Lucinda in a state of contemplation, hoping for clarity and reassurance amidst her apprehensions.

In the calm stillness of the night, Jake stirred from his sleep, sensing an unease that permeated the room. He turned to see Lucinda, her eyes open, staring into the darkness, a troubled expression on her face.

"Lucinda, what's wrong?" Jake's voice was soft, laden with concern.

Startled, Lucinda turned to face him, trying to mask the worry in her eyes. "I'm okay, Jake. Couldn't sleep," she replied, attempting to dismiss the gravity of her thoughts.

Jake could sense her hesitation. "Please, talk to me. I can see something's bothering you," he pleaded gently, reaching out to comfort her.

"You're worried about Amber. This has gone far too long, and it's unhealthy," Jake said

Lucinda turned and said, "I know, but the more I try to get the thought off my head, the more it returns. I have tried Jake, but it's not working. I don't want to lose Amber, and I don't want Amber to lose me; I don't want my daughter going through the same thing I went through after my parents died."

"You're immortal, Lucinda; you can't die," Jake assured

What if fate has destined for Amber's parents to die," Lucinda asked

"Okay, my wife has gone crazy; fate hasn't destined anything evil to happen, hey? This isn't the woman I married; don't let fear turn you into what you're not. I'm begging you," Jake pleaded.

"I will try not to let fear win over me, I promise," Lucinda said as she turned and closed her eyes.

Jake, though worried, respected her wish for solitude. He watched as she closed her eyes, pretending to sleep. Feeling less, he silently gazed at the full moon outside their window, an unspoken plea escaping his lips, "Please, the moon and Stars, help your child; don't let fear win over her."

With a heavy heart and a silent prayer for guidance, Jake settled back into bed, hoping for peace to envelope their home and soothe the anxieties that had gripped Lucinda.

◆ ◆ ◆

CHAPTER THIRTEEN

Little Amber tiptoed into her mother Lucinda's room, her wide eyes filled with wonder and innocence. "Mommy, do you think my grandparents Annalise and Phil will ever come back to life?" she asked, her voice conveying hope.

Sitting on the edge of the bed, Lucinda paused, her smile softening at Amber's question. She looked at her daughter, her heart swelling with a mix of emotions, memories flooding back. Her gaze was Amber's; momentarily, the room seemed to hold its breath.

"Sweetie," Lucinda replied gently, "life can be tricky sometimes. We don't always have answers to everything, do we?"

Amber furrowed her brow, contemplating her mother's words. "But if they do come back, how would you feel?" she persisted, her curiosity unquenched.

Lucinda's smile remained, but her eyes carried a hint of something more profound, a mixture of longing and acceptance. She placed a hand on Amber's shoulder, drawing her close. "If that were ever possible, I think I'd smile and say nothing at all," she said softly, her voice conveying mystery.

Amber pondered Lucinda's response, trying to decipher the meaning behind her words. Sensing her daughter's confusion, Lucinda tousled Amber's hair affectionately. "Sometimes, love, the most powerful feelings, are the hardest to put into words."

With a contented sigh, Amber nodded, feeling a sense of comfort in her mother's embrace. Lucinda's smile lingered, hinting at a story untold, a journey of love and loss that only time could unveil. She didn't want to think about anything that would end up dashing her hopes. How was she even going to explain to her daughter that she could still see her grandparents, all thanks to the newfound powers, and they would never be humans again? She didn't want to ruin her daughter at such a tender age.

Jake walked into the room. His face was etched with concern as he found Lucinda deep in thought. Sensing her unease, he swiftly approached her, concern evident in his eyes. Lucinda turned to him, a mixture of worry and confusion on her face.

"What's wrong, Lucinda?" Jake inquired, his voice tinged with concern, as he took her hands.

With a furrowed brow, Lucinda divulged, "Amber asked me something odd earlier—how I'd feel if my parents came back to life." Her voice held a trace of disquiet.

Perplexed, Jake's expression mirrored the confusion. "Where could she have gotten that idea from?" he pondered aloud, trying to decipher the reason behind Amber's unexpected question.

Looking slowly, Lucinda murmured, "I have no idea, Jake. It caught me completely off guard. She asked with so much happiness on her face, like it was something that would happen. How do I break it to her that people who are dead can never come back to life?" her concern was palpable.

Fearing that Lucinda might be growing anxious, Jake held her hands tighter, gazing deeply into her eyes. "Please, don't let this unsettle you; you don't need to tell Amber anything. Let her come up with her questions. As she grows older, the realities of this world will make sense to her," he urged, trying to calm her unease. "Amber and I will visit your grandparents, Maya and Greg, today. What if you come with us? Maybe being around family will help us understand what's happening."

"No, I'm okay; I still have some things to sort out here. You both should come back in time for dinner," Lucinda said

Jake looked at his wife and said, "Promise me you will be good. Remember, nothing will happen to her. She is just like us, and whatever she is displaying now shouldn't bother us, okay,"

Lucinda nodded in agreement, finding solace in Jake's assurance as Jake and Amber prepared to leave for Maya and Greg's place. An eerie feeling settled within her. An unspoken tension lingered in the air, an unexplained sense of foreboding that made her heart race faster.

Deep down, Lucinda couldn't shake off the unsettling feeling that something was amiss—something lurking beneath the surface, hidden within Amber's innocent words. It left her with a chilling sensation, a silent apprehension that lingered ominously in her mind. Something might have made her daughter ask that question, but she knows Amber is not one to force answers from her.

****

The Sun began its descent as Jake and Amber arrived at Big Grandma and Big Grandpa's house. The air filled with the warmth of family. Amber dove into playtime with Grandma Maya; her laughter echoed through the house.

As the evening progressed, Greg gestured for Jake to step outside momentarily. Concern etched on his face, Greg asked Jake if everything was alright. Jake nodded but shared his worry about Amber's peculiar questions regarding Lucinda's parents, Annalise and Phil. Despite her efforts to conceal her distress, he explained how it seemed troubling Lucinda.

With a comforting tone, Greg reassured Jake, "Kids ask lots of questions, Jake. The last time we were there, she asked us why Annalise and Phil didn't touch or play with her. We were shocked by the question, but we managed to reply. Amber is just curious. Lucinda will figure it out. It's tough, but she'll manage." His words carried a sense of understanding and wisdom.

Jake smiled, grateful for Greg's reassurance. "Okay, then," he replied, feeling somewhat relieved by Greg's words of wisdom.

Soon, Maya emerged from the house with Amber, who reluctantly bid goodbye to her grandma. Maya gently handed Amber over to Jake, a tender smile gracing her face as she wished them well on their way home.

"I love you," Amber said innocently as Maya and Greg replied, smiling.

As Jake and Amber made their way down the quiet streets, the Sun setting in the distance, a sense of tranquility enveloped them. Jake held Amber close, cherishing the bond between father and daughter. The streets, usually bustling with activity, now lay empty, painting a serene backdrop for their evening stroll.

In the peaceful embrace of the twilight hour, Jake and Amber walked hand in hand, the fading light casting long shadows across the pavement. Despite the day's mysteries and worries, the quiet stroll with his daughter brought a sense of solace to Jake's heart.

****

The serenity of the room was disrupted as Anya entered, her presence startling Lucinda. Anya observed d the troubled look on Lucinda's face, her eyes scanning her friend's worried expression.

"What's wrong, Lucinda?" Anya's voice broke the silence, tinged with concern.

Lucinda hesitated, unsure whether to divulge the complexity of Amber's recent revelation. "It's nothing g, just... thinking about Amber and her abilities."

****

At dinner that night, Amber, in her innocent curiosity, asked her mom and dad if they didn't want Grandma Annalise and Phil to be humans again. Lucinda stayed quiet, but Jake responded, "We'd love that, sweetheart, but it's impossible."

"When you say it's not possible, how do you mean," Amber asked curiously.

"They are dead, Amber; my parents died when I was still a child. During that time, I wanted nothing but to bring them back to life. I asked questions and did everything within my power, and nothing happened. So, when Daddy says it's not possible, believe him. We can't bring back dead people," Lucinda explained calmly.

Amber nodded. Her eyes filled with a child's understanding. "Okay, but Mommy, you and I don't have to believe in what people say is impossible," she replied, her tone accepting but still curious.

Jake looked at his daughter and asked what she meant, but Amber smiled happily and continued with her food.

Intrigued by Amber's sudden smile, Lucinda pressed, "Why are you smiling, honey?" But Amber grinned mischievously, knowing how to dodge questions like any four-year-old might. Lucinda attempted to maintain a serious tone, saying, "No more games, alright?"

After dinner, Amber dashed excitedly to her room, her parents trailing behind to tuck her in. Yet, as they leaned over to kiss her goodnight, Amber feigned sleep, stifling giggles as they left her room.

"Do you think she is up to something?" Lucinda asked as soon as she got to the room.

Jake looked at his wife and smiled. "What could a four-year-old possibly be up to at this time of the night? You worry too much about Amber,"

"She just said that we don't have to believe in everything people say is impossible," Lucinda replied

"Your parents are ghosts that we can see and touch once it's midnight. That is what others term impossible. So hey, Amber is right, let's sleep," Jake said as he pecked his wife.

Lucinda stared at the ceiling with different thoughts racing through her mind before she drifted off to sleep.

Once alone, Amber sat up, her imagination brimming with excitement. She glanced at the window and noticed the full moon casting its silver glow. It was exactly midnight. With a gleam in her eye, she stood on her bed and whispered some peculiar words that seemed to flow effortlessly from her lips.

"Thank you," Amber whispered to the stars outside, feeling a strange sensation coursing through her tiny frame. As she uttered those mysterious words, the stars twinkled and danced in a dazzling display, brighter and more vibrant than she had ever seen before.

"Don't worry, Mom, when you wake up by morning, you will be the happiest person ever," she said, giggling, content with her secret little ritual. Amber settled back into her bed, a satisfied smile gracing her lips as she drifted off to sleep as the stars twinkled in the night sky.

This moment marked another instance where Amber's mysterious abilities hinted at something beyond comprehension, leaving both her parents and herself unaware of the vast power she wielded. A child's innocent words whispered under the moonlit sky, invoking a shift in the world.

Lucinda stirred awake to tiny footsteps shuffling excitedly across the wooden floor. Amber's giggles filled the air, pulling her from the depths of sleep. Blinking away the remnants of dreams, Lucinda sat up, her heart pounding with curiosity.

"Mommy, wake up! I have a surprise for you!" Amber's voice bubbled with enthusiasm, tugging at Lucinda's hand.

Rubbing her eyes, Lucinda followed her daughter. A mixture of drowsiness and anticipation filled her. Amber led him into the sitting room, her tiny hand gripping Lucinda firmly.

With a flourish, Amber stepped aside, revealing figures standing by the window. The morning light illuminated their silhouettes. Lucinda's breath caught in her throat, her eyes widening in disbelief. Before she stood, her parents—Annalise and Phil—were alive and vivid as if plucked from a distant memory.

Shocked, Lucinda stumbled backward, her heart racing with a whirlwind of emotions. "How... How is this possible?" Her voice trembled, eyes darting between her parents and Amber.

Amber beamed, a radiant child's smile lighting up her face. She looked at Lucinda with a knowing innocence that belied her tender age. "Surprise, mommy! I found them in the pictures and brought them here!"

Lucinda's gaze darted from Amber to her parents, her mind struggling to grasp the inexplicable scene before her. Tears flew up in her eyes as she stumbled forward, embracing her parents tightly, feeling their warmth, and hearing their comforting words.

As Lucinda held them close, a flood of emotions surged within her—a mix of joy and disbelief. She glanced at Amber, overwhelmed by the inexplicable miracle her child seemed to have woven.

With a tender gaze, Lucinda looked at Amber, her voice quivering with emotion. "My darling, how did you...?" Her words trailed off, lost in the wonder of a child's imagination, realizing that sometimes, the innocence and magic of a young heart could create moments that defied all logic.

Jake emerged from the kitchen, and Amber dashed to him, laughing and joyful. "Did you wake your mom up?" Jake asked, his voice filled with amusement.

Amber giggled mischievously and nodded, "Yes!"

Curious about the commotion, Lucinda inquired, "What did you do, Jake?"

Looking surprised at himself, Jake explained, "I was shocked too. I could find Annalise and Phil this morning. In short, they're not ghosts anymore; they're human."

Everyone turned to Amber, eyes wide with astonishment. "What did you do, Amber?" Lucinda asked gently, trying to understand.

"I brought them back to life so I could play with them. Aren't you happy?" Amber replied innocently, her eyes wide with confusion.

Lucinda and Jake smiled warmly, assuring her, "We're delighted, sweetheart. Thank you."

They gently asked Amber to go to her room, wanting to speak privately. Alone together, Jake and Lucinda's faces lit up with joy and relief.

Lucinda hugged her parents tightly, a sense of happiness washing over him. "I think, Mom and Dad, I'm going to have breakfast with you for the first time. You died when I was 8. I didn't even know this was possible."

Lucinda's eyes welled up with tears of joy. "Yes, I'm here, Lucinda. We're all here now," Annalise said, holding her close, feeling an overwhelming sense of gratitude for this miraculous moment.

With tears of joy streaming down their faces, Jake and Lucinda embraced Annalise and Phil, their hearts flowing with happiness at the reunion they thought was impossible.

Amid the emotional embrace, Lucinda's words lingered in the air, marking a moment of importance in their lives—a breakfast together after years of separation caused by death, a symbol of the miraculous second chance they had been granted.

****

Amid the quiet midday, Annalise and Phil stood at the doorstep of her parent's home, exchanging glances filled with anticipation. As Annalise gently rapped on the door, a faint sense of nervousness mingled with excitement coursed through her veins.

The door creaked open, revealing Maya, her mother, her eyes widening in sheer surprise. "Annalise?" she stammered in disbelief etched across her face. It was a usual hour for her daughter to be present, especially considering their peculiar circumstances. She barely had time to process before Annalise rushed forward, enveloping her tightly.

"Mom, it's us!" Annalise's voice was filled with an undeniable joy. Maya was taken aback, still trying to comprehend the situation. "But it's noon. How...?" his voice trailed off, confusion and amazement intermingling in her words.

Before Maya could finish, Greg, her father, appeared behind her, observing the unexpected reunion. His eyes widened as he caught sight of Annalise and Phil, frozen in a moment of astonishment. "What's going on here?" His voice held a mix of concern and fascination.

Phil stepped forward, a faint smile playing on his lips. "Amber, she did something incredible. She found a way to bring us back to life," he explained, his tone tinged with disbelief as if even he was still coming to terms with their newfound humanity.

Greg's expression had shifted, a glimmer of hope mingled with disbelief in his eyes. "Amber? But how? It's impossible." His curiosity was palpable, a father's concern and fascination blending seamlessly.

Annalise chimed in, her eyes shining with unshed tears of joy. "Dad, Mom, it's true. We're humans again!" Her words hung in the air, a sense of surrealism enveloping the moment.

Greg's initial shock melted into an overwhelming wave of relief. Without hesitation, he pulled Phil into a tight hug, a silent expression of happiness for their salvation. Then, turning to Annalise, he embraced her just as tightly, his eyes glistening with tears of joy.

Finally reunited in this unexpected turn of events, the family gathered around the table for a long-overdue lunch. Laughter and conversation filled the air as they savored this precious moment together. Annalise and Phil shared stories of their ghostly adventures while Greg and Maya listened intently, their hearts filled with wonder at the unbelievable twist of fate.

As they relished each other's company, the hours seemed to slip away, lost in the joy of the present. It was a moment they had longed for, a simple yet profound reunion that mended the years of separation and uncertainty caused by their untimely death.

The sunlight streamed through the windows, casting a warm glow over the room as the afternoon waned. With hearts full and spirits soaring, they savored every minute, grateful for the unexpected miracle that brought them together once again.

As the afternoon drifted into early evening, the atmosphere remained charged with an indescribable warmth. Annalise, Phil, Greg, and Maya lingered at the table, reminiscing about moments long gone, sharing anecdotes from their ghostly and human experiences.

"Remember that time we got stuck in the body of the horses?" Phil chuckled, glancing at Annalise with a playful grin.

Annalise rolled her eyes, a smile tugging at her lips. "Oh please, it was hell, but I was grateful we could talk to Lucinda and share some time with her. Dad, you and Mom kept thinking Lucinda was insane, but she was just bonding with her parents."

Laughter filled the room, a harmonious blend of shared memories and newfound joy. Greg and Ma watched their daughter and Phil, their hearts swelling with contentment at the sight of their happiness.

"How did Amber manage to do this when Lucinda couldn't?" Maya's curiosity sparked a new wave of conversation, her gaze flickering between Annalise and Phil.

Annalise took a moment, gathering her thoughts before speaking. "It was a combination of things. Amber discovered ancient magic, though she won't say where, which she performed exactly at midnight today with the help of the moon, and here we are, Mom, as humans, not ghosts, not anymore.

Maya shifted close to her daughter and said, "Your death created a scar in our life, and your return today has somehow cleared that scar. Please don't leave us, Annalise; your mother won't bear it if anything happens to you or Phil again. Promise me that this return is for a lifetime,"

"I promise, Mother, I won't go anywhere," Annalise assured as she hugged her mother tightly. Tears flowed freely from their eyes as Phil and Greg watched with smiles on their faces.

****

Lucinda arranged the room, feeling a sudden breeze that whispered across her skin. "Anya, I know it's you. What is it? she questioned, sensing the familiar presence.

Anya's voice resonated softly, carrying a weight of revelation. "I hope you know what Amber did has granted immortality to your parents and grandparents," she conveyed, her words hanging in the air.

Startled, Lucinda clutched a vase, her heart pounding with realization. As Anya's words sank in, the vase slipped from her hands, shattering into pieces on the ground, mirroring the shattering realization of the enormity of Amber's actions.

Before Lucinda could respond, Anya continued, preempting her unspoken question. "Before you ask me how she did it, I don't know. When a child is from both worlds, I guess the powers she bears are more than the eyes can see. The truth is that Amber will do things that the world terms impossible," she explained, fading away into the ether, leaving Lucinda standing in stunned silence.

Jake rushed in, concerned, asking if everything was alright. Lucinda struggled to gather her thoughts, trying to explain. "It's Amber. It's something she did. We need to go to her room," she replied, her voice tinged with urgency and a sense of disbelief.

Jake could see the worry etched on Lucinda's face as she struggled to explain. "Amber did something when she brought my parents back to life. It involves making them and my grandparents both immortal," she managed to articulate, her voice trembling slightly with unease.

Concerned by Lucinda's distress, Jake gently urged her to calm down and share what had happened. Lucinda recited Anya's revelation, and in response, Jake surprised her with a probing question, "What are you so scared of, Lucinda?"

Feeling overwhelmed, Lucinda sighed heavily and sank onto the bed. "I don't know, Jake. I don't. I lost them when I was very young; I guess that messed up with my mind," she admitted, her gaze fixed on the world outside the window, lost in uncertainty.

Jake enveloped her in a reassuring hug, comforting her. "Our daughter's fate has already been decided. Whatever you do won't change that; if you try to alter it, there will be consequences that we won't like. Just let him be," he reassured, hoping to ease Lucinda's worry.

"Okay," Lucinda murmured, accepting Jake's reassurance and feeling more at ease.

Once Jake felt Lucinda had calmed down, he suggested they go and talk to Amber. Amber was found in the sitting room, engrossed in playing with the wooden toys Jake had bought her. Lucinda approached her gently, her heart full of apprehension.

"Amber, Mommy needs to talk to you," Lucinda said softly, trying to hide her concern.

Amber's eyes sparkled with curiosity as she looked up, eager to hear what her mom wanted to say, her innocent gaze fixed on Lucinda, waiting for an explanation.

Lucinda stared at the moon, which cast a gentle glow through the window, painting the room with a soft luminescence. Her daughter's innocent gaze held an unspoken wisdom as she explained the aftermath of her act of magic.

"Mommy, I made everyone who shares my blood immortal," Amber said, her voice tinged with the innocence of a child.

"What's immortal?" Amber asked, her curiosity shining through.

Jake, standing nearby, knelt, attempting to simplify the concept. "It means they won't ever die, sweetheart."

"I did it because you're sad," Amber continued, her voice tinged with a sense of understanding beyond her years. "You keep lying to yourself that you're happy but not."

Lucinda's heart skipped a beat at Amber's words, caught off-guard by her daughter's perceptiveness. "Amber, I.. "

"No, Mom," Amber interjected gently. "You would have done it long ago if you knew how. I want Grandma Annalise and Grandpa Phil to play with me, not just at midnight. And you want to hug and hold them, too. Do you think I don't know that they died when you were little?
I brought them back so you could play with them since you didn't get the chance to when you were little. I did everything for you, Mom.

Walking inside, Amber left Lucinda standing there, her thoughts swirling in a whirlwind of emotions.

Alone with Jake, Lucinda felt a wave of confusion and sorrow. "Amber is right. But it's not that simple, Jake. Bringing back the dead... I don't know if it's right."

Jake stepped closer, his voice a soothing balm to her troubled soul. "Lucinda, wouldn't you have done it if you knew how?"

Her heart heavy with the weight of past losses, Lucinda hesitated. "Their death has changed me. I thought I healed, but maybe I didn't. I know that I am the happiest person on earth right now that my parents are back to life, but deep down, I'm concerned about who I gave birth to. What kind of power have I unlocked on this planet."

"But now they're here," Jake said softly. "You and I are immortal, together with Amber; what's wrong with having your parents and grandparents turned immortal, too? We didn't know how, but Amber knows how, and she did it. It's not wrong to want that. You talk about the pain of your parent's death. I'm sure you wouldn't want to wake up one morning to hear that Maya or Greg is no more, and with the connection you have built with them over the years, their demise will wreck you."

Lucinda's eyes filled with tears as she realized the depth of her longing for her parents. Jake's words pierced through her inner turmoil, melting the icy walls she had built around her pain.

"You have been thinking about my grandparents, haven't you? Lucinda asked, and Jake nodded and said, "I also don't want them to leave, so I'm happy with what Amber did for them and our happiness."

Embracing her husband tightly, Lucinda let out a choked sob, the dam of emotions finally breaking. "I don't want to lose them again."

Jake held her close, his arms a sanctuary of comfort. "We won't. You're a family, immortal now. Let's cherish this gift Amber has unlocked for all of us."

In that embrace, amidst tears and unspoken words, Lucinda found hope. The magic Amber had unleashed had granted her parents and grandparents immortality and unlocked a path to healing the fractured pieces of their family, bridging the divide between the living and the departed.

THE END

MAIN CHARACTERS

Lucinda

Mia

Anya

Annalise

Phil

Grand Father

Grand Mother

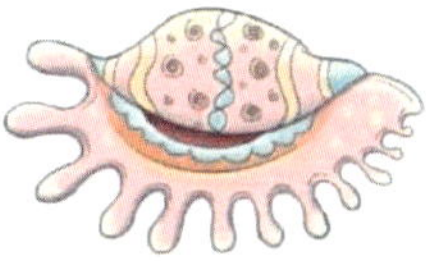

Elyon

Asgard

Amber

CREDIT

Annalise: **Mansi**
Amber: **Nicolette Bett**
Lucinda: **Chioma Rachel Chukwu**
Anya: **Natsyu "K"**
Grand Father: **Dennis WC Wong**
Grand Mother: **Jocelyn N. Wong**
Elyon: **Zarek Wong**
Asgard: **Kayin Wong**

Annalise's Dress Designer: **Neela** form SankalpArt

ABOUT AUTHOR

About the Author: Mr. Wong recently retired from Kaiser Permanente in Oakland, CA as a Nurse Assistant in the Operating Room Department and became a Licensed Vocational Nurse. It was only after exploring the paint sales industry that he felt drawn to pursue a career in healthcare.

Backed by an Associate of Arts in Retail Marketing from Chabot College, Mr. Wong earned a Bachelor of Science in Business Management- Personnel and Industrial Relations from California State University, Hayward. He was presented with the Albert Nelson Marquis Lifetime Achievement Award by Marquis Who's Who in 2020. Also, as a Sterile Processing Technician, Mr. Wong volunteers with Surgical Missions to Guatemala and Ecuador.

He owned a 1969 Ford Falcon Futura Sports Coupe. It has won awards at a couple of car shows and will be featured in a 2024 calendar. After retirement, he plans to travel and experience other cultures around the world.

◆ ◆ ◆

Made in the USA
Columbia, SC
09 April 2024

39e740d6-e2c2-479c-bc80-543763bc8b77R34